Another

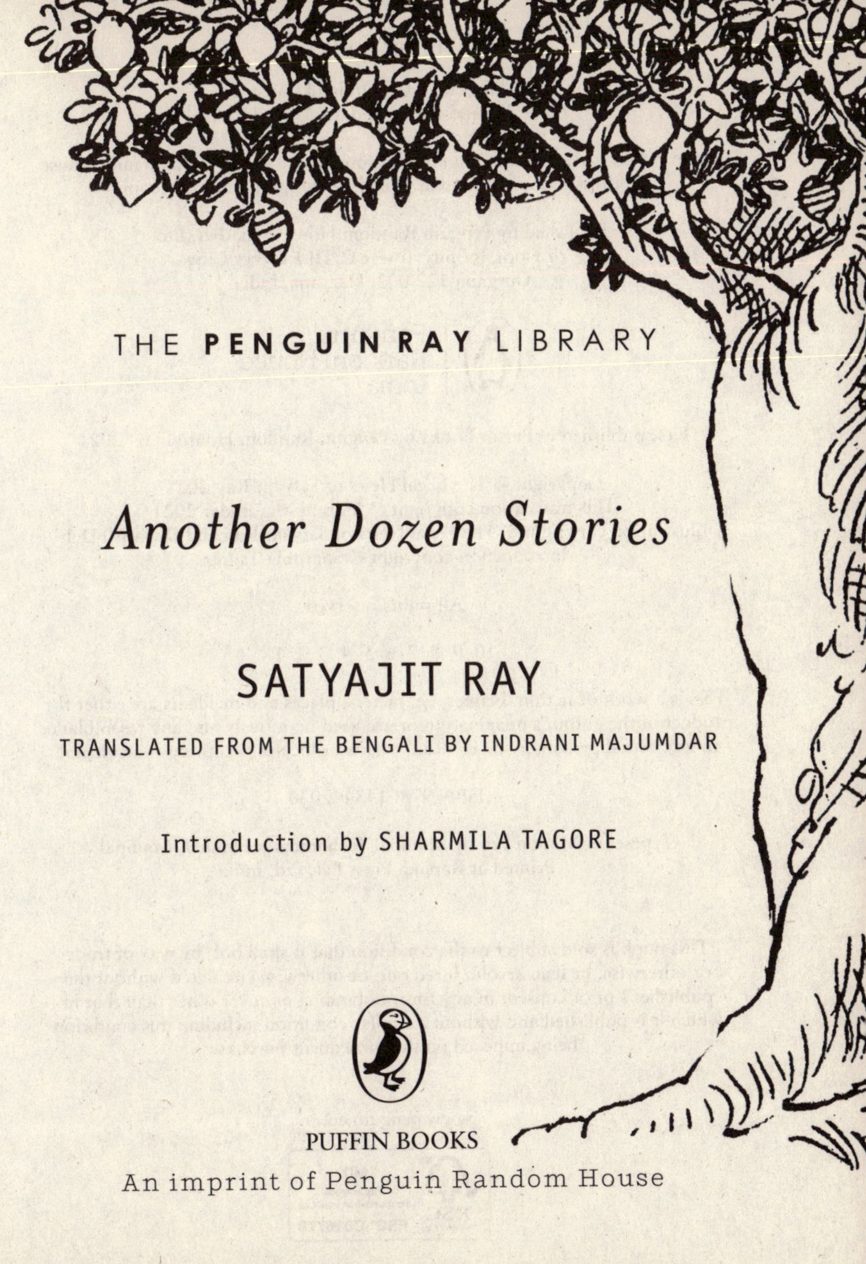

THE **PENGUIN RAY** LIBRARY

Another Dozen Stories

SATYAJIT RAY

TRANSLATED FROM THE BENGALI BY INDRANI MAJUMDAR

Introduction by SHARMILA TAGORE

PUFFIN BOOKS

An imprint of Penguin Random House

PUFFIN BOOKS

USA | Canada | UK | Ireland | Australia
New Zealand | India | South Africa | China

Puffin Books is part of the Penguin Random House group of companies whose addresses can be found at global.penguinrandomhouse.com

Published by Penguin Random House India Pvt. Ltd
7th Floor, Infinity Tower C, DLF Cyber City,
Gurgaon 122 002, Haryana, India

First published in Puffin Books by Penguin Random House India 2021

10 9 8 7 6 5 4 3 2 1

ISBN 9780143447030

Typeset in Minion Pro by Manipal Technologies Limited, Manipal
Printed at Replika Press Pvt. Ltd, India

www.penguin.co.in

Contents

Introduction

I was a young adolescent when Manik Da cast me in *Apur Sansar* and a year later in *Debi*. I have seen him engage with children, absorbing their every word, answering their every question, putting them at ease. It has been a fascinating experience.

Over the decades, I saw him creating some of the most captivating children's characters in cinema—Apu and Durga, Kajol, Ratan and Pikoo. His own sense of wonder and curiosity at the world around him reflected through these characters and in the stories he created for children. His complete understanding of a child's mindset, his ability to look at the world through the eyes of a child, was a rare gift he inherited from his family. His grandfather Upendrakishore Ray Chowdhury and his father Sukumar Ray were popular writers of children's books. In Bengal, their works are still seen as milestones in the history of children's literature. Manik-da carried this legacy forward, he revived the magazine, *Sandesh*, and added many more entertaining stories that appealed to children and to young adolescents.

He understood children's psyche, their inherent love for mystery and enchantment with the magical and sci-fi. In the process, he created two of the most enduring characters for young readers, Feluda and Professor Shonku.

It is such a joy to be able to revisit some of Manik-da's most memorable works in this genre. The stories translated by Indrani Majumdar highlight everything we have come to love and admire about Manik-da's multifaceted creativity. It's all here—the element of the unexpected, a hint of the supernatural, a whiff of the macabre with a generous measure of humour. This is a collection that makes me want to curl up in my bed with a pleasurable anticipation and let my imagination soar to the power of these timeless tales.

This is a befitting tribute to the master on his 100th anniversary.

Sharmila Tagore
March 2021

1

The Life and Death of Aryasekhar[*]

Many had expressed their opinion that Aryasekhar was a child prodigy. When Aryasekhar was only ten the last line of the first page of *The Statesman* caught his attention: *Today the sun rises at 6.13 a.m.* Carrying the paper with him, Aryasekhar went to talk to his father, Soumyasekhar.

'Father.'

'What's the matter, my son?'

'What have they written in the newspaper?'

'What have they written?'

'The sun will rise at 6.13 a.m.'

'Of course, they are quite correct. The sun rises exactly at that time.'

'Did you check your watch?'

'There's no need.'

'Why?'

---

* First published in the annual *Amrito*, 1968

'It's assumed.'

'How?'

'It's a matter of scientific calculation. Astronomy.'

'What if the sun doesn't rise at the right time?'

'The watch must be incorrect.'

'Suppose it's not incorrect?'

'Then what? Time for apocalypse?'

This marked the initiation of Aryasekhar's interest in scientific investigations. Two years later he approached his father with yet another query.

'Father.'

'Yes.'

'Are the moon and the sun the same in size?'

'Don't be stupid.'

'Then?'

'The sun is infinitely bigger.'

'How big?'

'By several million times.'

'Then why do they appear to be of the same size?'

'That's because the sun is much farther off.'

'The distance should be so precise that they appear to be of the same size?'

'Yes.'

'How did this happen?'

'No idea, really. After all I'm not the almighty.'

Here it must be mentioned that Soumyasekhar is not a scientist. He is a lawyer by profession.

After this conversation *with* his father, all that Aryasekhar could comprehend was that the apparent equality of the sizes of the sun and the moon was just an amazing coincidence. This hitherto unknown information created a major intrigue in his mind. Ignoring his textbooks, he opened his father's almirah, and taking out ten volumes of *Harmsworth Popular Science*, began to study the chapters on stars and planets. Needless to add, in this mission, he often had to turn to dictionaries for help. But this did not hold him back. A remarkable harmony of imagination and concentration in the boy helped him to carry on in his work.

On his fourteenth birthday, Aryasekhar opened a drawer of his father's table and took out three unused diaries. Choosing the largest one he wrote on the first page: *In my view, if any other living beings happen to exist in this solar system they can never be like us humans chiefly because there's nothing to match our sun or moon in those planets. In case there was, there would have been similar figures like humans. To me a human is a human only because of the presence of the moon and the sun.*

The following year, Aryasekhar, on a whim, began to verbally solve the trickiest of mathematical problems. Apart from the obvious problems involving addition, subtraction, multiplication and division, there were also problems which belonged to a rather advanced level of mathematics. For instance, Aryasekhar could guess the speed of a kite, its height from the ground level and the perimeter of the kite's flying area.

Aryasekhar's private tutor, Monilal Majumdar, could not reconcile to his student's brilliance in scientific matters. So out of sheer embarrassment, he decided to resign. Soumyasekhar too was at once amazed and alarmed to observe his son's conduct. Thanks to Soumyasekhar himself, and the initiatives taken by some of his friends and clients, a few reputed mathematicians of the city began to take notice Aryasekhar's unique abilities. The mathematics professor of Presidency College, Jibanananda Dhar, himself came and tested Aryasekhar for almost three-and-a-half hours using various methods, and left a glowing recommendation letter for him. In it he wrote, 'In his ability to solve these mathematical problems mentally/orally, I won't be surprised if Aryasekhar in no time surpasses Somesh Bose*. I wish this exceptionally talented youth a very long life.'

If the prospect of an added income beckons one, even a well-to-do person generally succumbs to it. Soumyasekhar was comfortably well off, but it wasn't really unnatural for him to be tempted to explore the possibility of an additional income by taking advantage of his extraordinarily talented son. But he had no plans to embark on such a mission without informing his son. He called for Aryasekhar.

---

* Somesh Bose was a great mathematician

'Well, I have been mulling over an idea.'

'What about?'

'With me—you know what I mean—the times we are facing now—one's not doing that well, getting by somehow. As we have observed such talent in you, the way everyone's praising you . . . doesn't it sound almost like magic? Suppose you showcase this talent to an audience—I mean after choosing a suitable venue with a well-organized . . .'

As he spoke, Soumyasekhar noticed an enraged, distressed look on his son's face. He felt ill at ease. He stopped talking for the moment and changed his tune to add, 'If, however, you have any reservations about this, no question arises.'

'Entertainment and talent are not the same thing, Father.' A question now crossed Aryasekhar's mind thanks to his father's suggestion. How can such an exceptionally talented son have a father with such a pathetic mentality? Was this polar opposite of attitudes between a father and son normal or was it an exception?

And if this was an exception, what was the scientific explanation behind it? There was no dearth of time in Aryasekhar's life because soon after discovering his mathematical genius, Soumyasekhar had taken him out of school. Aryasekhar now began an in-depth study on heredity and reproduction. Soon enough he discovered the significance of genes. In the genetic code present in each human being a few molecules indicate the nature, appearance and character of one's forefathers and of the future generations. How incredible!

Aryasekhar, once more, stood in front of his father.

'Father, don't we have a family tree?'

'A family tree? Why?'

'Do we have one?'

'Even if there ever was one, it must have been eaten up by termites. Why, do you think you are some sort of reincarnation? Or something similar?'

'No. I was thinking whether any predecessor in our family had been extraordinarily gifted. I know of you and grandfather. But prior to that?'

'Not a soul for the past seven generations. I can guarantee it. I've no knowledge of our history prior to that.'

After returning to his room, Aryasekhar plunged into deep thought. No gifted person in the last seven generations on my father's side. The same could be vouched for my mother's side—in fact the chances here were even more remote. Niharika Debi was a lady of very mediocre abilities. As she still referred to him as 'my boy', Aryasekhar made it a point not to go anywhere near her.

The influence of heredity was uncertain. Milieu? Environment? Can 33 Patuatala Lane be considered significant in this respect? Probably not. Then?

Can everything be proven simply on the basis of calculation? Father's father, his father—one can trace the very beginning of creation through a family tree. Hasn't the influence of genes been working since then? One wonders who and how were Aryasekhar's predecessors twenty thousand years ago? It was probable that one of them had drawn the picture of a bison on a wall of a cave in Altamira. Can't one speak of these prehistoric cave painters as belonging to the category of genius? Or the people who had planned a city like Harappa or Mohenjo-Daro? Or the writers of the Vedas and the Upanishads? If anyone of them could be traced as Aryasekhar's forefathers, there was no further reason for worry. Yet his mind was not at rest. He couldn't find any scientific cogency in the fact that a person like Soumyasekhar—so devoid of imagination, so grounded in the everyday world and so utterly dull—could be his father.

While fretting about this, a sudden thought struck him.

What if he was an illegitimate child? What if he had not been born out of Soumyasekhar's genes?

The instant this thought struck him, Aryasekhar realized that such a question could only be answered by his father and until he got the response he could not be at peace. That a son would question his father in the search for truth was to Aryasekhar just matter of course. Deeply immersed in a 926-page bulky law directory, Soumyasekhar initially could not even comprehend his son's question.

'Are you talking of a twin? Who are you referring to?'

'Not about a sibling. I want to know if I'm an illegitimate child.'

Hearing these words, Soumyasekhar's lips twitched. A trace of a quiver appeared between them. Soon that quiver spread throughout his body. And at that moment his right hand, which had been shaking, couldn't find anything other than a heavy paperweight. He picked that up and flung it straight in Aryasekhar's direction. Aryasekhar screamed in pain and collapsed on the floor with a bleeding head.

After his recovery it was observed that Aryasekhar had lost his supernatural power in mathematics. But he still retained his zeal for scientific research.

When Aryasekhar was nineteen years old, one evening as he was sitting under a sirish tree by the banks of the Ganga the droppings from a bird which was perched on the tree fell on his left shoulder. All of a sudden, he became aware of gravity. Typically, he began to research to educate himself further about this. He had earlier thought that the incident of Newton and the apple was an imaginary one. But after reading Newton's own writing in *Principia*, Aryasekhar changed his mind. Starting with Tycho Brahe, and moving on from Galileo to Copernicus, Kepler and Leibnitz, he finally reached Einstein. At Aryasekhar's level of education it wasn't easy to understand Einstein, yet Aryasekhar had an extraordinary knack of reading up all kinds of books—readable or unreadable, comprehensible or incomprehensible—from cover to cover. But in the present context, his eagerness was fixated on whether the last word had been said about the law of gravity.

After reading Einstein, though he could follow what exactly the law of gravity was, why was so much still unknown to him? He decided that this search for 'why' would now be his chief mission in life.

From that day, Aryasekhar decided he would pay attention to all trivial matters in life. He knew that insignificant incidents like the apple falling on Newton lay behind many discoveries.

Unfortunately, even after observing more than a thousand banal events over a period of three months he couldn't come across any incident whose scientific explanation had not already been recorded. Left with no choice, Aryasekhar had to look for a different strategy.

With the firm belief that one needs to immerse oneself in meditation before attaining knowledge he too decided to meditate. With this purpose in mind, he went up to the attic.

It was a Sunday. He went to the attic and sat down on a wooden cot. Just as he was about to shut his eyes, an insignificant scene on the terrace next door caught his attention through the open window. Their neighbour Phanindranath Basak's seventeen-year-old daughter, Dolly, had lifted her hands to hang her washed clothes on a rope. This scene, in the flash of a second, aroused in Aryasekhar's mind a fresh new angle to the law of gravity.

Within seven days he wrote down his observations in a 133-page article penned on foolscap sheets. It's not possible to fully describe his observation in this short biography, but he had noticed the following. Life itself is a protest against gravity because life force takes us to a higher plane whereas gravitation does the opposite. How did life at all evolve in spite of anti-life forces like gravity? The reason is the sun. But the sun's influence is not omnipotent. In the constant clash with gravity, the sun's influence, too, wanes. Consequently, the influence of gravity first strikes old age and finally death strikes life. In every sphere of human life—in its work, in its capacity for thought, in its sentimental outpourings—this opposition to gravity reigns supreme. All inferior qualities in humans, society's immoral practices, injustice, poverty, sorrow, distress and plans for warfare are all due to gravity. And whatever is striking, lively, prosperous and auspicious is credited to the impact of the sun. Due to the presence of gravity, the earth will never be free of mishaps. The earth would have been destroyed long ago, but the sun did not allow this to happen. Hence, destruction and creation have always existed simultaneously since time immemorial.

After completing this article, when Aryasekhar emerged from the attic he first acknowledged his gratitude to the sun and then to his neighbour, Dolly. At this precise moment their family retainer, Bharadwaj, informed him that his father had called for him.

Over the past few days Soumyasekhar had been worrying about his son. He had lost his wife Niharika the previous year. On her deathbed, she had lamented not having had the opportunity of seeing her son settle down.

Aryasekhar rolled up his papers and stood in front of his father.

'What will you turn out to be? A snake, a frog or an insect?'

'This can't be decided till the nature of my genes has been identified.'

'Whose nature?'

'Genes.'

'Half the time I can't follow you.'

'Not everyone can follow everything. Do I know anything about the legal profession?'

'Hope you follow that you survive today thanks to my profession. But at your age, it is not honourable to live off your father. So don't discuss genes or other such stuff with me. Whatever you do sitting in that attic, please remember that you are no better than any idler on the street. I give you a year's time. Please look for a job. As you are devoid of any degree, I don't expect much from you. But you ought to become self-reliant. Then the other task can be taken up.'

'What other task?'

'You ought to think about our lineage. Or have you decided not to marry?'

'Yes.'

'You will not marry?'

'No.'

'May I know why?'

'First of all, I've my doubts about my begetter.'

Soumyasekhar almost choked. Aryasekhar gave him time to recover his composure.

'Secondly when the influence of the sun is so crucial to my life, I don't need anything to impede my work or my deliberations.'

'Have you been initiated into some religious faith?'

'You may say that.'

'What faith?'

'It is my personal faith. A name is yet to be coined for it.'

For a moment Soumyasekhar had hoped that he may have solved the mystery of his son's unusual temperament.

Now he knew that it was not to be. He gazed at his son for a while. In particular, at his eyes. Did his looks reveal any sign of insanity? Soumyasekhar's great-grandfather, who had become senile in his old age, had once gone to the temple, where the entire village was gathered during Durga Puja, wearing no clothes. Not once had Soumyasekhar mentioned this incident to his son. A gentle compassion for Aryasekhar surfaced in Soumyasekhar. After all he was his only child—the only begotten. Let him be as he was—as long as he remains alive. And let him not lose his mind.

'It's okay. You may leave now.'

Aryasekhar had written that article in English—because he knew no Bengali reader would appreciate such a piece of writing. With inept hands and with much struggle he typed four copies of this article using his father's old Remington typewriter. After completing this task, he felt his entire body—hands, waist and back—had stiffened. Also, he felt suffocated after having stayed cooped up inside the room for so long.

Aryasekhar came down from the terrace. He decided to go for a short walk around Goledighi. As he left the house, he noticed a kurta-pajama clad white man with long hair, beard and moustache standing in front of his house looking around.

Noticing Aryasekhar, the youth came forward and inquired if he knew the whereabouts of the Mahabodhi

Society. Aryasekhar said, 'Come with me. I'll show you. I'm heading in the same direction.'

On the way, Aryasekhar came to know a little about this youth. His name was Bob Goodman. He belonged to Toledo, Ohio. He had abandoned his studies at the university and arrived in India in search of true love and enlightenment.

Aryasekhar took a liking towards this fellow. That very night he offered him his article to read. He commented, 'You're the first person to read this article. I'll eagerly wait for your feedback.'

The next morning, Goodman arrived munching peanuts and carrying the bunch of foolscap sheets inside his bag. He commented, 'It's great, great. Yeah—you got something there—yeah.'

When Aryasekhar thanked him in a soft measured tone, Goodman asked, 'Why is there so much pessimism in your writing? Many ways to overcome this issue of gravitation have been practised in your own country. Haven't you heard of levitation? Don't you know about the great yogis of your country?'

Goodman took out a packet wrapped in paper from his bag and gave it to Aryasekhar. It contained a sugar cube. Well, apparently it looked like a sugar cube! Goodman said, 'This indeed is a sugar cube but it contains a drop of acid. There could be no better way to capture gravitation than by consuming this stuff. Please give it a try. You'll go through stages of reactions—don't get scared. I feel this will help you overcome your pessimism.'

Carrying the sachet given to him by Goodman, Aryasekhar went straight to his terrace on the third floor. In the late autumn afternoon, against the backdrop of gentle sunshine, he sat cross-legged on a mat, put the sugar cube in his mouth and began to suck it.

Nothing happened for a couple of hours. Then at one point, Aryasekhar felt he was rising towards the sun. His body and mind seemed wrapped up in an indescribable state of intoxication. Looking down upon the dust-and-haze-wrapped Calcutta, he thought it looked like a Tehran carpet—vivid and colourful. The sky above him showed a wide range of numerous fragments spiralling upwards in motion. Aryasekhar realized these were kites but he had never seen such kites before. One such fragment came closer to him. In a gesture of friendly affection, Aryasekhar spread out his arms wide and surrendered himself to that object. After this he had no further recollection.

On Dr Bagchi's advice, Aryasekhar had to leave for Mihijam for a change of air to recover from ill health. Before his departure he took help from a professional typist and had fifty copies of his article on the law of gravity typed out and sent them to select scientists and scholars across the world. Among the individuals fortunate to receive a copy, a reply from one reached Aryasekhar's hands just a day before he left for Mihijam. The physicist Professor Carmichael, a Nobel laureate from England, had thanked him for the article and written: *I find it most intriguing.*

The post-Mihijam episode is a short one. Therefore, its description too is brief.

On 19 October, that is, a day after Aryasekhar reached Mihijam, he wrote in his diary: 'Birds birds birds birds. A bird is a bird. Most intriguing: Which living being reaches closest to the sun? A bird. O bird, how your flight flouts gravity!'

On 2 November, the retainer, Bharadwaj, saw that Aryasekhar had got hold of a weaverbird's nest from god knows where and, sitting on his bed with his legs spread out, was studying the pattern of the nest in rapt attention.

The next day, Aryasekhar gathered some straws and began to build a weaverbird's nest. That night his diary entry read: 'A man's highest achievement would be to rise to the level of birds.'

On 13 November, as his master was still out until late, Bharadwaj went out to look for him. After half an hour he found Aryasekhar lying unconscious under a babul tree next to a rice field. A weaverbird's nest was hanging from a spike on the tree.

Upon examination, the local doctor claimed it was sunstroke. Soumyasekhar arrived from Calcutta. After three days in a severe delirious state, Aryasekhar passed away in the presence of his father and the family retainer.

Before he breathed his last, Aryasekhar uttered only one word: 'O, Mother!'

2

Professor Hijibijbij[*]

I doubt if anyone will believe my story. But that doesn't bother me at all. Most people—unless they observe things with their own eyes—are rarely convinced about anything. Think of a ghost for instance. No, I am not going to write about ghosts. Believe me, I'm not sure how to define this incident in exact terms; yet the event has occurred in my life and is a part of my experience. Therefore, this is nothing but the truth and it is very natural that I would want to write about this.

Let me confess right at the beginning that I do not know the name of the protagonist who is central to this incident. He proclaimed that he has no name. He has also subjected me to an entire lecture on names. His opinions ran thus:

* First published in the annual *Anandamela*, 1972

'What's the big deal about a name, sir? At some point I did have a name. I've done away with it as there's no need for it now. Since you arrived here, met me, revealed your name, the question of a name arose. As no one comes here, there's simply no need for anyone to call me by a name. I've no acquaintances, I don't write letters to anyone, don't publish in any newspaper, don't sign on cheques—where's the need for a name! I have a retainer who happens to be mute. Even if he wasn't mute, he would not have used my name; he would have referred to me as 'Babu/Master'. End of the matter! Now the question is how you will address me. That must be bothering you . . .'

Finally, it was decided that I would call him Professor Hijibijbij. In due course I shall reveal why. Let me first get back to the beginning.

It all happened in Gopalpur. Situated on the coast of Bay of Bengal in Ganjam district, ten miles away from Beharampur, Gopalpur is a small coastal town. Over the past three years, due to work pressure, I had not been able to take any leave. But this year I had finally obtained three weeks' leave and decided to travel to this town, I had heard much about but had never visited. Apart from office work, my other job is that of a translator. I have translated seven crime fiction works from English to Bengali. According to my publisher, these books have garnered a good response in the market. It is to some extent on his insistence that I availed of this leave. The responsibility of translating an entire book during this period rested squarely on my shoulders.

I'd never been to Gopalpur before. On the very first day I realized that I had made a good choice. I'd rarely been to such a quiet yet picturesque place. It was quiet particularly because it was the off season, the month of April. The crowd that usually comes here for a change of air was yet to arrive. At the hotel where I was staying, there was just another guest, an elderly Armenian, Mr Aratune. He was staying in a room at one end of the hotel facing the west end and I was at the east end. The beach began right below the long verandah of the hotel. Within hundred yards the waves hit the sand. Red crabs often climbed into the verandah and loitered around. Sitting in a deckchair, I enjoyed the scene and worked at my writing. In the evening I walked along the beach for about two hours.

On the first two days I went in the westward direction, following the coastline; on the third day I thought I should check out the eastward direction as well: I found these weather-beaten seafront houses very interesting. Mr Aratune mentioned that these houses were perhaps 300 to 400 years old. At one time the Dutch had set up a colony in Gopalpur. These houses apparently belonged to that period. The houses were made up of bricks that are small and flat, what's left of the windows and doors are gaping holes and as for the roof, nothing is left of it.

I did check out a house once from the inside; it seemed rather gloomy.

After reaching the eastern side I saw the shore had expanded and therefore the city too seemed to have receded further beyond the sea. At least a hundred upturned boats were lined up in this area. I realized that the 'nuliyas'—the local fishermen and bathing guides—used these boats to catch fish. I noticed a few nuliyas were gathered in groups in different directions; some young nuliya children were catching crabs on the seashore and a couple of pigs were grunting about aimlessly.

Amid this I also noticed two elderly Bengali gentlemen sitting atop an upturned boat. One of them, wearing glasses, was having a tough time trying to fold up a newspaper against the strong breeze. The other one, with hands folded and pressed against his chest, was gazing earnestly at the sea, smoking a bidi. When I went near them the man with the newspaper inquired in a friendly tone, 'Have you just arrived?'

'Yes, just two days earlier.'

'Staying at the "Sahib" hotel?'

With a faint smile, I asked, 'Do both of you live here?'

The gentleman holding the newspaper had finally managed to control it. He replied, 'I do. I have been living in Gopalpur for twenty-six years. That New Bengali Hotel belongs to me. Ghanashyambabu, like you, is here for a change of air.'

When I was about to move on after saying 'Very well', another question was flung at me: 'But where exactly are you heading in that direction?'

I said, 'Just like that . . . only for a stroll.'

'Why so?'

What a bother! Did I have to justify where I was heading?

Meanwhile, the gentleman stood up. The light too was dimming. A dark blue cloud seemed to have formed in the north-west direction of the sky. Was there likely to be a storm?

The man continued, 'There would have been nothing to worry had it been a couple of years ago. You could have walked in any direction without any fear. Since last September, however, on the eastern side, a few miles away, well beyond the nuliya quarters, a strange individual has settled down. You see those ruins? That creature lives in one of those houses. I, of course, haven't been to the house. Our local postmaster, Mohapatra, says that he has seen him.'

I inquired, 'A mendicant?'

'On the contrary!'

'Then?'

'I don't know what he is. Mohapatra said he has filled up all the cracks and holes of the building with tarpaulin. No one knows what takes place inside. People have seen purple smoke billowing out through an opening on the terrace. Even though I haven't been inside the house, I have seen the fellow a few times. Once, he was passing by in front of me right here. He was dressed in a yellow coat and pantaloons. His face was devoid of any moustache or beard but he sported thick curly hair. As he walked, he kept mumbling something to himself. I even heard him laugh out loud once. I spoke to him. But he did not reply. He is either rude or insane. Perhaps both. He has a domestic help also living in the house. You can spot him shopping in the markets in the morning. I have never seen such a robust and hefty man. He has a crew cut and his built was stubby. Quite like that pig there. That fellow is either mute or keeps his mouth shut. Doesn't talk even while shopping. He communicates with the shopkeepers through hand gestures. It is perhaps sensible not to venture anywhere near a house with a servant like that, whatever bizarre traits the owner might have.'

Ghanashyam too had stood up now. After throwing away his bidi on the sand, he said, 'Let's move.' Before they both left in the direction of their hotel, the manager told me that his name was Radhabinod Chatterjee and he would be delighted if I dropped by his hotel for a visit.

Having translated thrillers for years, mystery attracts me naturally. This is something that the manager of the New Bengal Hotel would never be able to understand. Not once thinking of returning home I continued in the eastward direction.

It was now ebb tide. The water had receded. Waves too were few. Near the shore, where the waves turned into foam, a few crows were jumping around. Just when the foam glided ahead and then receded, the crows approached the foam and began to peck at the bubbles. After leaving the nuliya quarters behind, and walking for another ten minutes, at a distance I saw what seemed like a red sheet moving along the expanse on the wet sand. It left me a bit startled. Coming closer I realized it was a ring of red crabs. As the water had receded, each cluster was marching towards their habitat.

Walking for another five minutes I finally spotted the house. As I had already heard about the tarpaulin patchwork, I had no difficulty in identifying it. But nearing it I gathered that not only tarpaulin, but bamboo, wooden planks, rusted corrugated tin and even pieces of pasteboard had all been put to use to repair the house. Having observed this closely I realized that unless rainwater seeped through the terrace it was not quite impossible for anyone to live here. But where on earth was the fellow?

After I had stood there for a couple of minutes it crossed my mind that if indeed the fellow was crazy and if he really had a brawny attendant, it wasn't very wise of me to be gaping at the house with such abject curiosity. Instead, how about ambling along casually and moving a bit farther away? After having arrived this far how could I retreat without even catching a single glimpse of this fellow?

Engrossed in my thoughts I suddenly noticed something moving in the darkness behind the gap of the front door. Soon, a dwarf-like man emerged from the door. I understood right away that he was the owner of the house. Taking advantage of the darkness, he had been observing me for some time.

'Oh! I notice six fingers on your hand!—heh . . . heh!' Out of the blue a soft, thin voice reached my ears.

This was true indeed. Since birth I've had this extra finger attached to my thumb in one of my hands. It doesn't really serve any purpose. But how could this gentleman have observed this from such a distance?

When he came closer to me, I noticed that his hand held an ancient one-eyed binocular. I bet he had been studying me with this.

'That one must be the thumb's little brother? Isn't so? Ho . . . ho!'

The timber of his voice was almost absurdly thin. I had never heard a voice like this coming from such an elderly figure.

'Why don't you come in—why stand outside?'

I was seriously startled. After hearing Radhabinodbabu's description, a different image had formed in my mind; but now I found the person rather jovial and welcoming.

The man was standing ten feet away from me. I could hardly see him in dusk's fading light, and I was immensely curious to observe him closely. Hence, I didn't refuse his invitation.

'Be careful, you're a tall man, and my door is a bit . . .'

Crouching in order to protect my head, I finally managed to enter his shelter. The raggle-taggle house gave off an old misty smell mixed with that of the damp ocean and an entirely unknown odour.

'Come to the left. On the right—heh . . . heh—is my study.'

A gap on the door to the right was tightly sealed with a large piece of cardboard. We entered the room on our left. One could perhaps call it the drawing room. In one corner was a table on top of which lay a few big bulky journals and books, three fountain pens, an inkpot, a bottle of glue and a large pair of scissors. Opposite the table lay a rusted tin chair, next to it stood an upturned packing case and right in the middle of the room was a huge chair. This last item could have rightfully belonged in the drawing room of a royal family. It was built of a solid wood with superb inlay work, and the seat was wrapped in deep red velvet decorated with a floral pattern.

'You may sit on that box while I sit in this chair.'

This was my first moment of doubt. Even if he was not stark raving mad, the man was definitely rather temperamental. Otherwise, how could someone invite a guest into his house and offer him a packing box while he himself perched on a throne?

Yet, watching him in the evening light coming in through the gap of the tarpaulin fixed on the window, I noticed no signs of insanity in his eyes. In fact, his face radiated innocence and gaiety. That's precisely why despite his weird request I was not annoyed with him. I sat down on the packing case.

'Now tell me,' the gentleman said.

What did I have to say? I had not come here to say anything; only to observe. If you're expected to speak apropos of nothing, it can annoy you. Therefore, I introduced myself abruptly . . .

'I'm from Calcutta; at present here on a vacation. I am a writer. My name is Himangshu Chaudhury. I was sauntering around this area and your house caught my attention.'

'Very well. So happy to hear about you. But I have no name.'

Another moment of misgiving. What did he mean by having no name! All of us have a name. Why should there be an exception in his case?

When queried on this he launched into a sermon on names. When he finally wound up and saw me silent, the gentleman smiled wryly and said, 'I don't think my words satisfied you. Then let me say one thing—I have decided on a name for myself on my own. Of course, I haven't disclosed it to anyone but as you possess six fingers, I've no hesitation in telling you.'

I gaped at him. The light inside the room was getting dimmer now. Why could I not spot the servant? At least a candle or kerosene-lit lamp should be brought inside the room.

The fellow suddenly tilted his head in one direction and said, 'Have you noticed my ears?'

So far I hadn't but when my attention was drawn to them, they startled me.

I had never seen such ears on a human being in my entire life. Instead of being rounded off, the upper portion was pointed—just like in dogs and jackals. How was this possible?

After displaying his ears to me the man performed yet another amazing act. He pulled at a tuft of his hair and it landed on his hand. In complete awe I saw that other than the top of his head and around his ears there was not a single strand of hair on him. With this new appearance, complementing his quiet countenance and his impish grin, in an instant a name sprang out of my lips: 'Hijibijbij.'

'Exactly!' The fellow clapped his hands and burst into a giggle. 'If need be, you can even match it with the picture.'

I said, 'No need. The image of Hijibijbij has been ingrained in my mind since childhood.'

'Well, well, well. If you wish you can happily use this name. In fact, if you add the prefix of a professor, it'll work even better. But please don't divulge this to the others. If you do so—heh . . . heh . . . heh . . .'

For the first time since entering the house I felt a touch of fear. Without doubt he was definitely eccentric. Or maybe even mad. It is very difficult to understand such an individual. You needed to be alert for what he'd blurt out next or what action he'd take.

The silence between us had become uncomfortable; hence I said, 'It seems that the colour of the pointed part of your ears is different.'

'That has to be,' the gentleman replied, adding, 'it doesn't belong to me. My ears weren't quite like this when I was born.'

'In that case, are the ears also artificial like your hair? Will they come off like your hair if you pull them?'

The gentleman burst into a chuckle once more and said, 'No way . . . no way!'

Oh no! The fellow *was* insane. I said, 'Then what's that?'

'Wait. First let me introduce my retainer to you. You may find him familiar, as well.'

I hadn't noticed any other presence till now. God knows when another fellow had appeared and was standing near the back door. He carried a kerosene lamp. It was the servant I had heard about from Radhabinodbabu.

When the gentleman signalled to him the servant quietly entered the room and placed the kerosene lamp on the table. Really, I doubt if I had ever seen such a well-built man in my entire life. He was wearing a striped top and a short dhoti. You couldn't help but be impressed looking at his well-rounded calf, strong hand muscles, powerful wrists, broad chest, and the wide girth of his neck. Yet he wasn't above five feet two inches tall.

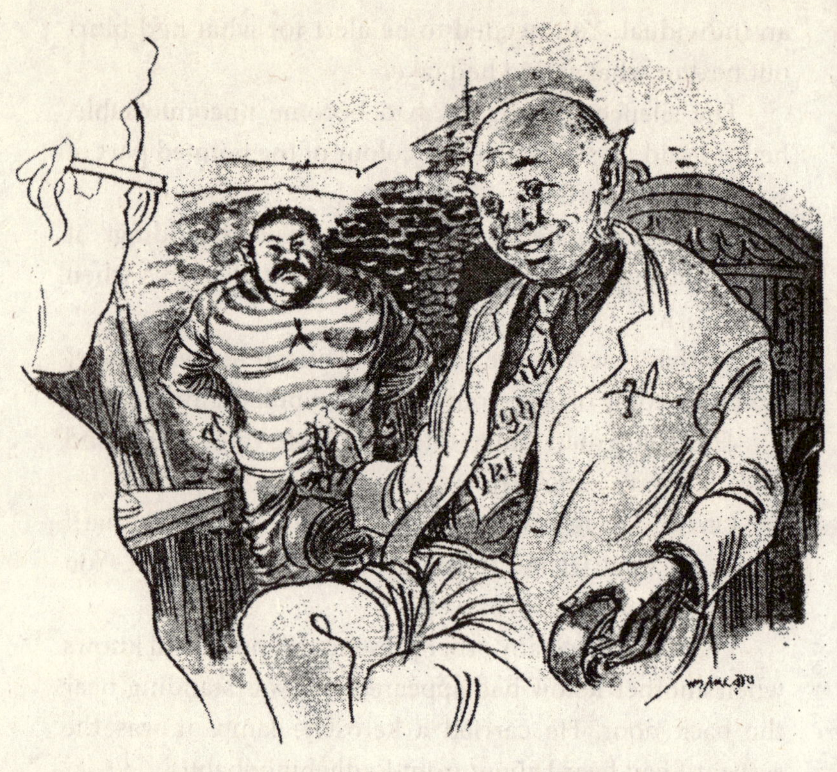

'Does my servant remind you of someone?' asked Hijibijbij.

After putting down the lamp on the table, the servant looked at his master, waiting for further instructions. After I had watched him for a couple of minutes it suddenly clicked why he looked so familiar. In amazement I said, 'Oh, yes! He is none other than Shashthicharan!'

'Spot on! Spot on! In sheer joy the gentleman began to dance even while seated.

Our Sasti Charan, just for fun, keeps elephants to toss around
He clocks a hundred hundredweight, his thews are truly ironbound

'Well, he doesn't weigh nineteen quintals but a bit more than three-and-a half quintal. Certainly this was so in 1967. I'm also not sure about juggling an elephant, but ever since he arrived here I've seen how each morning he juggles with a pair of wild boars in his hands. And this chair of mine—he carried it here with only one hand.'

'From where?'

'Ho . . . ho . . . ho . . . ho . . . must you hear that? Shashthi, please go and fetch two tender coconuts for us.'

Shashthi left to carry out the order.

I could hear a thunderstorm brewing outside. The tarpaulins began to wobble in the strong gusts of wind. If I didn't leave, I would be in trouble.

'Didn't you ask about my ear? That one, actually, is a combination of the ear of a wildcat and my original one.'

I found this too funny. I said, 'How did you fuse the two?'

The gentleman said, 'Why, if a heart of a human can be transplanted into another human, why can't one half of an animal's ear be affixed to a human ear?'

'Were you a practising doctor before this? Something along the lines of plastic surgery?'

'Yes, of course. Why just in the past? I still practise. Heh . . . heh. But this was no ordinary plastic surgery. For instance . . . that extra thumb of yours . . . in case you didn't have it, it would have been no big deal for me to add that on too.'

I tried very hard to imagine this fellow as a senior doctor but just couldn't do so. Yet I felt very strange every time I glanced at his ear. His patchwork seemed too seamless.

The chap said, 'Other than medicine and science books I've read only two other books in my entire life—*Abol Tabol* and *Ha-ja-ba-ra-la*. And in these two books what appealed to me the most was the mention of these creatures referred to as weird and peculiar. People simply laugh off things happening out-of-the-box as improbable. It is just not fair. In my childhood I used to suck on candles, do you know that? I loved it. And the flies I munched on—countless.'

He paused as Shashthicharan had just returned with the tender coconuts. He placed two enamel glasses on the table and kept a coconut on each. He pressed each one with his palms and they split up easily. Then he poured the water into the glasses. Shashthicharan handed over the glasses to us.

Taking the first sip my host said, 'Do you know why I specialized in plastic surgery after studying medicine?'

'Why?' My curiosity had now doubled. I was anxious to check on the range of his imagination.

Hijibijbij continued, 'Because watching those images were not enough. I often thought . . . what if such animals actually existed. I had no doubt that they did. But I wanted them inside my room, near my hands, in front of my eyes—do you understand?'

I said, 'No, sir, I don't understand. What are these creatures you're talking about?'

'Well, for instance, storcoise, porcochard, gizzard.'

I said, 'Yes, understood. And then?'

'What then? I started with the gizzard. I had both components with me: a parakeet's head and a lizard's tail. Just as they are mentioned in the original text of *Abol Tabol.* It worked out beautifully! I could join them with great ease. But you know what?'

Looking a bit upset he paused for a while and said, 'The creature didn't survive too long. It refused to eat anything. How could it survive without any food? What the book mentions is nothing but the truth—but even if the bodies match, the minds don't tend to bond very well. Thus, instead of experimenting on this head-body fusion, I've involved myself in another kind of experiment.'

The fellow suddenly seemed to grow absent-minded. Thank god for the coconut! Had it been tea and biscuit I wouldn't have dared touch it. God knows where Shashthicharan had disappeared. I could hear some kind of clattering noise. It seemed to be coming from the room the fellow called his study. Perhaps the door was being opened.

Violent winds blew outside. I didn't quite fancy the rumbling noise of the clouds. I couldn't linger here any more. I needed to get back to my work. I stood up after thanking the gentleman.

'Leaving? But I needed to discuss something with you.'

'Tell me.'

'You know what—I've assembled almost everything . . . a porcupine's thorn, a goat's horns, a lion's hind legs, a bear's fur . . . the entire assortment. But part of it also requires a human element—it ought to resemble that original picture, doesn't it? It would be of enormous help if you come across such a human figure.'

Having said this he unearthed an old copy of *Abol Tabol* which lay under his papers and notebooks, opened a page and held it in front of my eyes. A very familiar picture indeed. Clutching on to a club a rather strange creature was glaring at the running figure of a harmless man.

Oh don't be scared—please don't be scared! I don't intend
to beat you.
Believe me, if we fought a bout, I never could defeat you.

'Won't it be just wonderful if I could create such a being? It's not much really—my collection is almost ready, I've already affixed the latter part of the body, all I need now is a look-alike of this human figure.'

I said, 'Do humans have such protruding eyes?'

'Certainly!' The gentleman almost jumped up defensively. 'Eyes are always round! As the eyelid covers most of the eye it doesn't show the roundedness.'

I proceeded towards the door. To sum up, he was mad, obstinate and also a chatterbox.

'That's fine, Prof. Hijibijbij, I'll let you know if I come across someone like that.'

'Yes, you must. It will help me to no end. I, too, am looking around. You never told me where you've checked-in?'

Pretending not to hear the last bit I stepped out in the dark. And began to run. I don't mind getting wet but the sand which the wind raises messes up your face. Somehow managing to cover my face and shielding my eyes, I finally reached my hotel. By then it had already started raining. When I switched on the light, I saw that it was not working. As I was about to go out into the verandah to call for help I realized there was no need for it. A bearer was coming towards my room carrying a candle. When I inquired, he said that it was normal for Gopalpur to go without electricity every time there was such violent rain and storm.

After having my dinner at 8, when I settled down to write, I found it difficult to concentrate. My mind kept wandering towards Professor Hijibijbij. How on earth was this man living in this 300-year-old crumbling patchwork house? It reminded me of that decrepit ancient shrivelled old lady from *Abol Tabol*! Unless one is absolutely crazy, can anyone really do so! And Shashthicharan? How on earth had he found a creature as hefty as a bull! Is he really cooking up something weird in that east-facing room? How much are his stories sheer cock-and-bull and how much are they for real? One could have brushed it all aside as pure bunkum, but what was disturbing was that pair of ears! Clearly it wasn't just a cut-and-paste job. By the light of the kerosene-lit lamp I had noticed blisters in the pointed part of one of his ears. Which proves that those ears are in fact part of his body; and like the rest of his body they also have veins, nerves, blood circulation and the works.

Well, the more I think the more I feel that if it weren't for those pair of ears I would have felt far less perturbed.

When I got up at 5.30 the next day I noticed that overnight the clouds had vanished. Over my morning cup of tea it struck me that the meeting with Hijibijbij was rather amusing. It had actually been nothing—late in the evening, under the half-lit kerosene lamp, what I had seen was only a partial view and perhaps partly it had been my imagination. Even after my return to the hotel it had been dark. However, I couldn't shrug off the lingering doubt in my mind. This morning when I looked at the sun and the serene sea, I thought that the man was nothing but a crackpot.

Close to my foot, near the ankle, I felt a mild throbbing pain. On examining it, I noticed a small cut. Something like a shell had probably scratched my foot while I had been hurriedly walking back. As I had not brought any iodine or Dettol along with me on this trip, at around 9 a.m., I headed towards the market.

The road towards the market takes you to the New Bengal Hotel. In front of the hotel's verandah I saw Ghanashyambabu, whom I had met yesterday, checking out corals being sold by a vendor. Hearing my footsteps the gentleman looked up and at that instant my heart missed a beat.

It was the same face right out of the pages of *Abol Tabol*—the face the madcap Prof. Hijibijbij was hunting for!

Yes, there was no doubt—long strands of white moustache flying in two directions below that squat nostril; protruding veins on two sides of his long neck just as in the drawing; even that goatee with a few strands below his flat chin. No idea why though, perhaps because I didn't like his manners, I had never looked at his face carefully yesterday. We did exchange glances and I also greeted him with a namaskar, but the gentleman simply didn't bother to acknowledge my presence. How very rude.

Yet I was worried about him. There was no way I wanted him to fall into the clutches of this crank. If Hijibijbij or his retainer spotted him, they would undoubtedly whisk him away to that battered house. And god alone knows what would befall him there.

I decided that I'd meet Radhabinodbabu on my way back from the market and explain everything to him. I'd caution him to keep an eye on the only guest in his hotel.

However, while buying Dettol I abandoned the idea. Why should Radhabinodbabu believe such outlandish stuff? What's worse, he might think I was off my rocker. It might also offend him that I had gone ahead and met Hijibijbij in his house despite his warning.

On my way back, when I looked at Ghanashyambabu once again, another thought crossed my mind—to me he might appear to bear a striking resemblance to that illustrated figure, but to Hijibijbij it may not be so. Therefore, my fears could well be unfounded. It would perhaps be wise not to discuss this with anyone and certainly not to utter a word to the professor about Ghanashyambabu either. Now on I'll go on my walks strictly in the westward direction and the rest of the time I'll devote myself to writing in my own room in the hotel.

Soon after my return the bearer reported that a gentleman had come looking for me. As he couldn't meet me, he had left a letter instead.

Written in a very tiny handwriting the letter is reproduced here:

Dear Mr Double Thumb,

You must come to my abode this evening. The thorn of the porcupine and the fur of the bear have been seamlessly fastened to the rear part of the lion. An ideal cudgel has also been acquired. The three horns are awaiting the head. Therefore, we are now looking for the head and the pair of hands. Shashthicharan has brought news of a certain individual, who bears a remarkable resemblance to that original sketch. I sincerely hope my experiment will be a grand success today. Hence, I'll be forever grateful if you set your foot in my 'House of Paradoxes' residence.

Sincerely yours

HBB

I remembered that Hijibijbij had decided to name the house in *Ha-ja-ba-ra-la*, 'Paradoxicality'. After reading the letter my worries returned as I could strongly intuit that Shashthicharan had indeed spotted Ghanashyambabu.

I tried to concentrate on my writing in the afternoon. A stormy wind began blowing in the evening. Sitting on a deckchair my mind relaxed while looking at the sea from the verandah. The wind from the north-west direction was blowing through the waves and the foams atop the waves were breaking out in various directions. How lovely it all looked.

Around 6 o'clock I suddenly saw Radhabinodbabu walking along the beach in a somewhat dishevelled state. He stopped in front of my verandah. Reaching closer, he spoke breathlessly: 'Have you seen my guest walking in this direction?

'Who? Ghanashyambabu?'

'Oh yes. He was to wait for me where we had been sitting yesterday. Now I do not see him here. There's not a soul nearby with whom I can check. On top of this a problem cropped up in my hotel. I've lost my gold watch. I got delayed as I was cross-examining my servant. But he hasn't come by in this direction, perhaps?'

I stood up from my deckchair.

'No, not this direction,' I commented, 'but something is making me suspicious. We may get news of him if we go to a particular place. Is the stick you're carrying sturdy enough?'

Perplexed, Radhabinodbabu asked, 'The stick? Oh yes . . . that stick belonged to my grandfather . . . hence . . .'

I had nothing in my possession—on the first day of my visit I'd bought a pair of Korat fish teeth. I clutched it in one hand and picked up my torch in the other.

Since we were heading in the eastward direction, Radhabinodbabu asked in a heavy voice, 'Are we going beyond the nuliya settlement?'

'Yes. But not very far. A few miles.'

On our way he repeated the same sentence thrice: 'I just can't figure out a single thing, sir. I'm so completely clueless.'

Walking along with an elderly person, on a sandy path, it took me over an hour to cover one-and-a-half miles. Dusk had already settled by then. Till you get really close to the house there's no way you can make out if there's anybody inside it. Radhabinodbabu's enthusiasm kept dwindling as we neared the house. When we were a couple of metres away from the house he suddenly came to a halt and asked, 'What exactly is on your mind?'

I said, 'Since you've come all the way what's the harm in proceeding a bit further?'

Left with not much choice the gentleman continued to walk behind me with some reluctance.

After reaching the house I had to switch on the torch as it was pitch-dark inside. Like the previous night the kerosene lamp should have been lit but it hadn't been.

When we entered the house through the front door, the first thing we saw in the light of the torch was a man lying face down on the floor. However, the fellow wasn't dead as his wide chest was still heaving heavily.

'Oh! This is that servant,' said Radhabinodbabu in a rasping voice.

'That's right. Shashthicharan.'

'You seem to know the name, too!'

Paying no heed to this comment I headed towards the drawing room. The room was empty. There was no sign of the professor. Then we moved towards the study.

The door was half ajar. We could enter it only after stepping over Shashthicharan.

The room was just as big as the drawing room. On one side atop a table was a pile of paraphernalia—bottles, knives, medicines, et al. A strong smell hung heavy over the room. I'm familiar with this odour. I have come across it standing outside animal enclosures in the zoo.

'Oh dear, I can see the gentleman's kurta here,' Radhabinodbabu suddenly shouted.

I too had noticed the kurta on him this morning. It was a brown kurta with three-quarter sleeves and white buttons down the front. There was no doubt that it belonged to none other than Ghanashyambabu.

As he inserted his hand in one of the pockets of the kurta, Radhabinodbabu heaved a sigh of relief—though he still looked jittery given the eerie atmosphere. He had found his gold watch.

'But tell me, what exactly is happening here? What are these things lying around? The kurta is here, the watch inside the pocket is intact but where is the fellow? And where did that oldie go?'

I answered, 'It's clear that there is nobody inside. Let's get out.'

Shashthicharan was still unconscious. Once again, we jumped over his body and walked out to the beach. Looking towards the sea in this darkness I spotted a human figure. He was coming towards us. When he reached closer, I flashed my torch at him. It was Professor Hijibijbij.

‘Is that Mr Double Thumb?’

‘Yes, sir, I’m Himangshu Chaudhury.’

‘Couldn’t you have come earlier?’ He inquired in a tone of deep regret.

‘Why so?’ I asked.

‘He has gone! I got such a picture-perfect human. Within an hour the fastening procedure was completed and he then walked around effortlessly, spoke very clearly and as Shashthicharan looked frightened, he flung the club at his head and then finally advanced straight towards the sea. I thought of calling out to him but as he has no name, how could I? . . . A human head, lion’s legs, porcupine’s back, pair of goat’s horns . . . Yet I can’t quite fathom why he proceeded towards the water . . .’

Still chattering, the gentleman stepped inside his spooky house. Until now the torch in my hand had been focused on him but when I lowered my hand, I noticed footprints on the sand. Fresh footprints. No, not quite footprints; rather pawmarks.

Following the marks and focusing the light on them, I went ahead. In due course the marks seemed even deeper on the wet sand. Going over the crab nests, over the countless shells, the pawmarks eventually reached the water and then disappeared into the depths of the sea.

Finally Radhabinodbabu opened his mouth.

'I can now gather my wits. This chap is completely insane; you're half insane but whatever happened to that swindler guest of mine?'

I threw away the Korat fish teeth into the water. As we began to walk back towards the hotel, I said, 'Why don't you request the local police to take up this case? As the kurta has been found here, ask them to start their investigation from this very location. But what I dread is the police officer ending up in the state I'm in—'a state of paradox!'*

---

* What a wonderful time I had translating this hilarious tale bordering on the bizarre. Yet what did cross my mind was the question: Will everyone be able to find this equally entertaining? Primarily because the story is so generously peppered with allusions and linguistic quirks that it adds another layer to its rich wit and quaint humour. To anyone familiar with Sukumar Ray's seminal works, *Abol Tabol* (Stuff and Nonsense) and *Ha-ja-ba-ra-la* (A Topsy-Turvy Tale), it becomes an easy task to connect, but what about those who are not?

We come across Satyajit Ray's references to his father's literature in a few of his films, particularly in the Feluda movies, *Sonar Kella* (*The Golden Fortress*) and *Joi Baba Felunath* (*The Elephant God*). But in this inimitable story, Ray engaged in a very clever ploy to pay a personal tribute to his father, Sukumar, by adding various references found in *Abol Tabol* and *Ha-ja-ba-ra-la*. And what joy it gives you to connect these allusions and inferences.

The name of the nameless protagonist of the story, Professor Hijibijbij, is an 'alive and credible' character from the 'Carrollian fantasy' *Ha-ja-ba-ra-la*. He is followed by his close associate,

Shashthicharan, a very impressive figure from the poem 'Paloan' (The Strong Man) in *Abol Tabol*, whose description has never failed to impress a child. Continuing with his eccentricities, the professor confesses with much glee to sucking candles and munching flies, which will be quite familiar to those who have read 'Danpite' (Daredevil/Infant Joy). This too makes an appearance in *Abol Tabol*. And then appears the much-familiar double-barrelled creatures storcoise, porcochard, gizzard from the poem 'Khichuri' (Stew Much). Next is the mention of the intimidating character that remains nameless—the strange creature clutching on to a club glaring at a running figure of a harmless man. This incredible image will forever daunt and haunt me or anyone who is familiar with the poem 'Bhoy Peona' (Don't be Scared/The Invitation). The professor's seamless operations of different 'beings' is obviously inspired from the ham-handed doctor in 'Haturey' (Doctor Deadly). Even the ramshackle house described throughout is nothing short of a 'character', but in this story it smacks of the old lady's cut-and-paste house, 'Burir Bari' (The Old Lady's House), which again can be located in *Abol Tabol*. In the original, the house is called 'Kingkortobyobimuroh' (flummoxed/paradoxical) and it comes straight from the house mentioned in *Ha-ja-ba-ra-la*, which unfortunately came tumbling down all too soon!

The English translations are all taken from the impeccable translations by Sukanta Chaudhuri (*The Select Nonsense of Sukumar Ray*) which Ray himself endorsed as 'admirable . . . able and imaginative'.

3

Poisonous Flowers[*]

I

'Don't go in that direction, Babu!'

These words startled Jaganmaybabu. He had not realized that there was anyone else in the vicinity. Hence, he was alarmed. He now noticed that on his right, a couple of yards away, stood a teenaged boy wearing blue-striped shorts and covered in a green shawl. The boy was dark in complexion; with neatly brushed hair, and calm yet sharp eyes. Even though he was a village boy he definitely seemed to go to school. An illiterate child would never look like this.

'In which direction should I not go?' asked Jaganmaybabu.

'That way.'

---

* First published in *Sandesh*, 1977

While on his walk, Jaganmaybabu had stopped to look at a particular site. It must be what the boy was referring to.

'Pray, why should I not go? What will happen if I do?'

'There's poison.'

'Poison? Where?'

'In that tree.'

To be honest, Jaganmaybabu had paused in his walk just when he'd spotted that tree. A flowering tree. Probably wild flowers. A few yards away from the main road stood a solitary tree on a patch of raised land. There were no other trees nearby. This tree was waist high. It had small conical leaves and within the folds of the leaves were beautiful flowers in shades of violet, orange and yellow. Jaganmaybabu was particularly surprised because despite walking down the same path for the past three days he had not noticed this heap and the tree on it. It was another matter that while walking one needs to pay more attention to the pathway especially if it's an unfamiliar and difficult one.

Therefore, it wasn't surprising that he had missed the tree.

The lad was still standing and gaping at him.

'What's your name?' asked Jaganmaybabu.

'Bhagwan.'

'I see! How did you learn Bengali?'

'In school.'

'Why were you following me?'

'And that's my house.'

Jaganmaybabu noticed that about a quarter of a mile from the mound, adjacent to a bamboo clump, stood a tiled roof hut. He looked in the direction of the boy once more. He wanted to ask him a few more questions. Why should the boy all of a sudden forbid him to do something?

'What's the name of the tree?'

'Don't know.'

'How do you know it's poisonous?'

'But one dies.'

'Who dies?'

'Snakes, frogs, rats . . . birds . . .'

'How do they die? When perched on the tree? Or by eating those flowers?'

'If you go anywhere near it.'

'How close?'

'A couple of metres.'

'You are quite one for tall tales. Or are you already a ganja addict? Check such facts with your teachers at school. A flowering bush can never be poisonous.'

The boy continued to look at him. In complete silence.

'I'm new here. I've come here for a change of air. I'm not too well. Do you understand? Please don't tell tales like this. No one's heard of such a plant in this part of the world. It cannot exist.'

'It's not from this land. A sahib got this.'

The lad seemed incorrigible. He was hell-bent on convincing me.

'Which sahib?'

'He lived in the same house you're staying now.'

'When did he come here?'

'The year before the year of drought.'

'What's his name?'

'No idea. Red face. Golden hair.'

'He came and planted that tree on this mound?'

'Don't know.'

'Then?'

'The tree came up soon after the sahib left. You see that forest. He wandered about there with a piece of glass in his hands.'

The sahib might have been a botanist, Jaganmaybabu thought. This boy was speaking of such remarkable stuff.

'Just look at this,' the lad said, pointing at something next to the mound. 'You see that stone, right beside that.'

Jaganmaybabu looked closely. He could see a white object.

'What is that?'

'A snake.'

'A snake?'

'It was once a snake. It was a snake with stripes. It's a skeleton now. It died. The flowers exhale poison.'

Jaganmaybabu fixed the binoculars on his eyes. Yes, a snake indeed. The skeleton of a snake. He now looked at the flower through the binoculars. It did not look as simple as it had earlier. None of the colours looked plain. There was a splash of mauve on yellow; violet on yellow; black and white on orange.

Putting the instrument to his eyes once more, he spotted another dead creature. This one too was a reptile but it had four legs. Possibly a kind of chameleon. It too seemed to have died a few days ago.

'Haven't they become alert by now? They still come over here to die?'

'Every day they die—one or two.'

'But I don't see too many. There are only two.'

'There are some behind the mound. When these carcasses grow in number they are dragged out and cleared with the help of a bamboo stick.'

'Who clears them?'

'My father and I.'

'In that case why don't you strike the tree with the bamboo and simply uproot it? That would put all trouble to rest.'

'It grows back.'

'What are you saying?'

'Even after it's burnt down it grows back.'

Jaganmaybabu didn't want to pay much attention to this affair. He was still not quite convinced. Not even a fraction. At the same time, he partly believed in this as he had once heard of carnivorous plants. There were so many amazing things in the universe humankind was unaware of.

'Are there any more such plants here?'

'Yes.'

'Where?'

'In the forest.'

'Is this the only one in this area?'

'Haven't seen any other, Babu.'

If all this was true, one had to admit that apart from exposure to such sylvan surroundings, as well as fresh delectable food, Jaganmaybabu stood to gain something more. This wasn't something he had expected at all. He would have something to talk about when he returned to his office. Poisonous flowers. Poison in the tree's breathing. If he hadn't observed those two dead creatures, he wouldn't have believed the boy at all. But then why should the boy make up such stories? A practical joke of this nature was possible in the city, particularly on 1 April. Being a diehard city dweller, Jaganmaybabu could feel that such a thing could never work in a village. He also felt that it was the most memorable day of all the forty-two years of his life. For the first time ever he had come to learn about poisonous flowers.

But what amused Jaganmaybabu was that he had initially had no plans to visit Kathjhumri. He had gone to Daltonganj to spend a fortnight with his sister. Since the previous year he had begun suffering from breathing trouble. The doctors—and not just the doctors, even other people familiar with him—had been suggesting that he spend a few days in a dry climate. 'You have never married. Who are you saving all your money for? Try to spend it. If not on us, certainly on yourself.' This 'all your money' situation had suddenly appeared like a huge tsunami in his otherwise sedate life. After visiting the racecourse for three continuous days, on the fourth day, he had won the jackpot. All at one go. It was a princely sum of Rs 64,000. Yet he had never paid any attention to a horse; never read a single page of any book on racing. He had gone there only on the request of a friend. And partly out of curiosity. Doctor Nandy thought that the asthmatic attacks had begun only after he received that money. It was possible. Jaganmaybabu himself had observed that with this sudden turnaround in his fortunes certain other changes had come into his personality as well. Under normal circumstances he had been much more generous but as of now he had become more astute with his money. He could afford to buy a car, yet he didn't. He had plans to give a lavish treat to his friends but landed up offering them only sweets. On the birthday of his dear nephew, Tilu, after bargaining for a toy train for Rs 44, as he was taking out his money, he finally decided to purchase a train which cost only Rs 27. When the idea of taking a break did strike him his friends were too happy to suggest various options for places, hotels, tourist lodges, something which Jaganmaybabu could easily afford. But at the last moment, simply to keep costs low, he decided to visit his sister in Daltonganj. He had planned to stay there during this entire period. But as both his nephews became afflicted with chickenpox, his brother-in-law suggested, 'Why don't you check out Moor Sahib's bungalow in Kathjhumri? It's like an English cottage which offers accommodation and good food at a reasonable price. You'll be able to experience a wonderful change as well as have a place to rest. The sahib is no longer there—he died four months ago. But his wife lives there. I know they rent it out to guests.'

The elderly Mrs Moor didn't raise any objection. But she also added, 'My husband looked after all arrangements. He had his fixed clientele but I haven't received any letters or telegrams from any of them. I've no problem in letting out a room for you but I can't give it out for beyond a fortnight. Sorry about that.'

'There will be no need for more than that.'

After staying in Daltonganj for three days, Jaganmaybabu shifted to the sahib's bungalow on a Friday, and had been there for the past three days. He soon realized that for a person of his temperament there couldn't have been a better place than this to enjoy his holidays. The first advantage was the weather. Not once had he suffered from any breathing trouble since he arrived here. Secondly, the Calcutta-bred Jaganmay Barik could not have imagined how a place which had no tram, bus, lorry, taxi, radio, television, cinema or human cacophony could work as a wonderful tonic. He could now apprehend why Calcutta people were often so insular. Only after arriving in Kathjhumri had he understood what relaxation was all about.

The very first glimpse of Moor Sahib's bungalow instantly cheered up Jaganmaybabu. He could see the mountain range both in front and beyond the building. Closer to that was a forest range beside a level of uneven land surrounded by variety of knolls. And near that stood a tiled cottage with a chimney—much like an English picture postcard—surrounded by a line of tall trees. After crossing the verandah one reached a room that was neat and tidy in appearance, with minimal furniture. When he noticed the design of the curtains across the door and windows, it dawned on Jaganmaybabu that getting to stay at such a bungalow for a holiday was no less a fortune than winning a jackpot at the racecourse.

Soon after arriving there, Jaganmaybabu had chalked out his daily schedule. After waking up and having his tea he went for a morning walk and on returning he settled down to his breakfast. This was followed by sitting in the verandah or in the compound in front to read magazines. He had brought twenty-five copies of *Reader's Digest* from his sister's collection. This was followed by a bath, lunch and finally an afternoon siesta. In the evening, tea was once again followed by a stroll. Dinner at 8.30 p.m. was followed by sleep.

That day, soon after his return from the morning walk, he asked the chowkidar, Banwari, about the poisonous flowers. Tactfully he began with an introduction instead of broaching the subject directly.

'Do you know of a boy name Bhagwan?'

'Yes, Babu. Bhikhua's son.'

'Who's Bhikhua?'

The chowkidar said Bhikhua worked as a labourer at Chowdhury Babu's wood warehouse.

'Near a road towards Bhagwan's house there's a particular flowering tree. The tree emits poison into the air. Do you know of it?'

'Yes, Babu.'

'Is this true?'

'They all die—snakes, rats, insects.'

Banwari put down the plate of bread and omelette and went to fetch the teapot.

When Banwari returned, Jaganmaybabu asked him, 'Did any sahib come here three years ago?' Banwari said many sahibs had come here earlier. There was a time when Moor Sahib came here every winter with his wife. Banwari could not recall if any other sahib had visited three years ago.

Jaganmaybabu decided he'd visit the market in the evening. The baazar was in Pannahat, about two miles away. The railway station too was located there. To reach there one needed to take a cycle rickshaw from the station. You could catch a direct train from Pannahat to Daltonganj. On the first day after his arrival he had visited the market. He'd made friends with two Bengalis. The postmaster, Notubihari Majumdar, and another individual, Pabitrababu, who was staying at the Royal Hotel. Jaganmaybabu had met him while looking for a sweet paan. Pabitrababu said he had visited Kathjhumri earlier as well. He worked as a medical representative. According to him, Royal Hotel was a hotel only in name.

It was more like a three-star inn. Pabitrababu seemed quite a jolly fellow. He was probably around thirty to thirty-five years of age.

'Where have you checked in? There's no other place in Kathjhumri where you can stay. Do you know anyone who works for the Chowdhury Company?'

'No, sir. I'm staying at Moor Sahib's bungalow.'

'Oh! That cottage surrounded by infant trees.'

Jaganmaybabu remarked, 'It's certainly surrounded by trees but not sure if these are infant trees. If you look carefully, they look quite senior—heh heh. Well I'm a completely city person. At the most I can identify mango, banana, coconut and banyan trees—I'll be in trouble if you ask me anything beyond these.'

Jaganmaybabu resolved to check this out with Pabitrababu and Notubihari as well. The chowkidar's confirmation was not enough. In fact Jaganmaybabu planned to write about this poison tree when he returned to Calcutta. So far no one had written about it. In this regard he would be a pioneer.

Notubihari had little to add on the subject. He said, 'Well, sir, I was transferred here just a year ago. You won't get much local news from me. You should rather check with the others.'

From the post office Jaganmaybabu headed towards the market. He needed to buy some betel leaves and also an exercise book if possible. He ought to prepare himself to write about this matter. He had a pen but had not brought a notebook with him.

He came across Pabitrababu in front of the teashop. Sitting on a bench, Pabitrababu was reading a Bengali newspaper. He said, 'Come on over. Have some tea. Bharadwaj, two cups—two, instead of one.'

'Have you heard of poisonous flowers?'

Pabitrababu folded the newspaper and looked up at Jaganmaybabu. 'Yellow, orange, violet? It's on the right side on your way to Talhar's? On the top of a mound?'

'You seem quite well informed.'

'I told you—I've visited this place four times already. I've noticed this for the past two years. The first time round, I also saw the body of a piglet lying next to it.'

'Is that so? How come you haven't told anyone about this? You come from Calcutta . . . in the newspapers, media—?'

Pabitrababu laughed. 'What's there to say, sir? Nature can play truant in so many ways. Do papers cover everything? God knows how many such breeds of poisonous flowers, poisonous fruits, poisonous insects and poisonous birds exist in this world? Well, sir, I live in Calcutta where the air itself is poisonous. With each breath you lose out on five seconds of your life—I read about this somewhere. Who cares about poisonous flowers, sir?'

'But for the local crowd . . . for them at least it's a cause of real danger.'

'Just don't go anywhere near the tree. It's safe if you stay a few metres away from it. Everyone here is aware of this.'

Jaganmaybabu got up soon after finishing the tea. It was now middle of October. Soon after sunset, the temperature dropped immediately. It was best not risk catching a cold.

By the time Jaganmaybabu bought his notebook from a stationery shop right next to the teashop and returned to the cottage it was 6.15 p.m. He felt rather excited. Having gathered all confirmed facts, he could easily start writing. If this write-up attracted the attention of botanists, it would serve a real purpose. People would also get to know about the place, Kathjhumri. Was the tourist department aware of the place? He didn't think so.

Since he had absolutely no practice in writing, Jaganmaybabu opened the notebook and rested the tip of his pen against his chin. He continued to sit in this posture for half an hour. It yielded no result. Writing wouldn't come so easily. He still had ten days left of his stay. He had to give himself more time and room for thought. Poisonous flowers . . . Jaganmaybabu repeated it twice to himself. Poisonous flowers! People could not help but read eagerly on such a subject.

II

Today there was no need for binoculars. When he reached the mound at seven in the morning, from the road itself, Jaganmaybabu could clearly see with his naked eyes the dead body of a rabbit. The carcases of the snake and the chameleon were still visible. Bhagwan or his father would probably come to clear them once there were a few more bodies.

Jaganmaybabu tried to calculate how far the tree would be from the main road. Ten metres? Thirty? He was sorely tempted to go closer to the tree and study it carefully. It was probably fine as long as he did not go within a couple of metres.

What if that lad's estimate was not correct?

What if the impact of the flower reached out beyond two metres?

Jaganmaybabu took three steps on the grass but retraced his steps immediately. Snake, rabbit, chameleon, pig. The boy had not said anything about insects. Grasshopper, ants, mosquitoes, flies—did these too die from the tree's poison? Or were they spared? What about large creatures? He had to be certain of these facts before he began writing. Today he couldn't spot that boy. Should he return home? He'd like to interview the boy once—just as newspaper men do with many people.

When this idea dawned upon him Jaganmaybabu also thought—there was no need to rush. Everything would work out in its own time, own pace, own rhythm. He still had seven days to go.

The water was excellent here. It worked wonders for the appetite. Thinking about his breakfast he returned to the bungalow. The large compound was encircled by a bamboo fence. There were two wooden gates—one on the westside and the other on the north side.

On a wooden plank set in the northern gate—from where Jaganmaybabu has just entered—the name of Mr Moor could still be read. The path from the gate ended right in front of the verandah. Those large trees which Pabitrababu had referred to as infant trees could be seen behind the cottage. On the southern front, there were two large trees, unfamiliar to Jaganmaybabu. He did not know their names. Among these, the tree that was a little farther off had well-spread-out branches and twigs. If its trunk had been dark, he could have spotted it more easily but despite that, the tree next to it didn't escape his attention.

That same tree with those strange flowers. Poisonous flowers!

Jaganmaybabu's appetite vanished like magic. That tree had not been there yesterday.

Jaganmaybabu had asked Banwari to fetch him a deckchair and he was basking in the sun seated a couple of metres away from the white tree trunk. He had no work other than enjoying that charming autumnal sunshine. His eyes wandered all around surveying the surroundings including that white tree trunk. He certainly remembered that because he had thought about the colour of that trunk resembling that of a eucalyptus tree. He was familiar with this one tree. Eucalip—

What's that?

A bird.

Brown in colour—from head to the tip of its tail. Smaller than the size of a house mynah. The bird was pecking and eating something from the ground and occasionally looking up to chirp. All within the range of five metres from the white tree. And now, leaping a few times, the bird reached closer to the tree. Not waiting any longer Jaganmaybabu loudly clapped his hands twice. Letting out a sharp cry the bird flew away. Jaganmaybabu heaved a sigh of relief. But the tree still remained there. Couldn't one do something about it? There were plenty of boulders lying about on the road.

Picking up one Jaganmaybabu threw it at the tree. The tree trembled. It had struck! But would just one boulder work?

Jaganmaybabu felt blood rush to his head. He aimed thirty boulders towards the tree. As he had never played any cricket in his life most of them missed the tree. But a few struck. The tree had now bent low.

'It'll stand up again, Babu.'

Bhagwan. Clutching a book in his hand he stood outside the gate with a grin on his face.

'Let it stand up,' said Jaganmaybabu. A momentary relief at least.

Bhagwan left.

When he turned his head towards the bungalow, Jaganmaybabu realized that both the chowkidar as well as the gardener had observed the incident. It was clear that both were shirking their duty. Couldn't they have come up to help him?

While having his breakfast, Jaganmaybabu thought that perhaps he himself was to be blamed for the chowkidar and the gardener's indifference. He should have tipped them soon after arriving. The gardener had come to fetch him from the station. Mrs Moor had informed him via a telegram. Instead of a coolie he had loaded his luggage on the gardener's back. A suitcase, a bedding and a large flask with a tap attached. He had himself walked on carrying only an umbrella and a pot of sweets his sister had given him.

After reaching the bungalow, he had taken out a couple of rupees to give to the gardener but had put it back in his pocket. He thought, 'I'll compensate him when I leave. Let me first check on the quality of their services.'

Both of them had worked well for him. But beyond their call of duty they hadn't gone out of their way to chat with him or to find out if he had any special needs. Neither of them had ever inquired whether he was facing any trouble or discomfort. Only on this account had the stay at Kathjhumri turned out to be 'less than perfect' for him. But now he felt that he was himself also partly responsible for this.

'Are there any similar trees around the house?' Jaganmaybabu asked the chowkidar while stirring sugar into his tea. The chowkidar said that this was the first time he had noticed the tree within the precincts of the bungalow.

'Did it grow overnight?'

'So it seems, Babu.'

'Just keep an eye on this. If you see something please let me know.'

Before Banwari could say anything, however, Jaganmaybabu noticed it. He had just stepped out into the verandah after his afternoon siesta.

From the eastern side of the verandah, at a distance of about ten metres, a bunch of familiar flowers could be seen popping up. The flowers were swaying in the gentle breeze.

Jaganmaybabu could feel his hands and feet turning numb. Somehow, he dragged himself away and sat down on the cane chair. He did try to call out to the gardener but no sound emerged from his throat. His throat was parched. His head spun. His hands and feet felt clammy.

A mild wind was blowing from the east. From the direction of the tree. In other words those flowers were puffing out that poisonous air . . .

Jaganmaybabu could think no more. He could sit no more. He was again having trouble breathing.

Mustering up the limited strength at his disposal, he somehow managed to get up from his chair and stumbled across the drawing room to reach his bedroom. He then lay flat on the bed.

When the chowkidar came to inquire about his dinner he said, 'Nothing for me—I've no appetite.'

In spite of that, Banwari got a glass of warm milk for his babu. After much persuasion he could manage to drink only half a glass and returned the rest.

Drums played somewhere in the distance. In the market, he had heard about a forthcoming fair. Santhals would be performing a dance. God knows what time it was now. Jaganmaybabu felt cold even under a blanket. He took down a wrapper from the dress-hanger and added another layer to the blanket. It worked. In a while, Jaganmaybabu could feel his eyelids getting heavy.

Up until now, Jaganmaybabu had enjoyed uninterrupted sleep every day of his vacation. But not so tonight. The light that greeted him when he opened his eyes alarmed him but he remembered that he himself had instructed Banwari to keep the kerosene lamp on in the room. It was still very cold. The breeze had to be coming in from the window. But he had shut it before going to sleep. Had someone opened it?

Jaganmaybabu craned his neck to check.

The dressing table was right next to the window. The kerosene lamp on it shone its light on the window shaft.

Not just the shaft. Also on something else sticking out from outside. One could easily identify the object in this light.

It was the tree. The same tree. Those familiar flowers. Yellow, mauve and orange.

Poisonous flowers.

Jaganmaybabu could sense an anguished howl trying to emerge from his lower belly and travelling through the windpipe. When it finally came out from his mouth he would pass out.

And that's exactly what happened.

Jaganmaybabu had been relieved to get the compartment just to himself. Primarily because he did not feel like interacting with any fellow human. Over the seven-hour journey he was trying to contemplate how his divine three-day stay in Kathjhumri could have turned into such a tale of horror over the last two days. But as the guard blew his whistle a familiar figure entered his compartment. The postmaster of Pannahat, Notubihari Majumdar. Jaganmaybabu had not come across this gentleman since their initial meeting.

'What's this, sir? You're already returning? Or are you also going to Betol?'

'Betol?'

'The next station. There's a fair. I'm going shopping on my wife's orders.'

'Oh, I see.'

'Where are you headed?'

'Daltonganj.'

'Are you not feeling well? You look so pulled down in just these two days.'

'Hmm . . . just a bit low . . .'

Notubihari nodded his head and said simpering, 'Ah! That gentleman's luck is with him.'

'Luck?'

'I'm referring to Pabitrababu.'

'Why?'

'Well, it's been ten years that he has been staying in Moor's cottage at least twice a year. He has almost monopolized it. In October and in March. He goes there to write. He is a well-known writer after all. Pabitra Bhattacharjee—aren't you familiar with the name? He also teaches Bengali to a boy named Bhagwan, a woodcutter's son. A tutor by choice. An idealistic man in some ways. He'll be delighted to hear that you've left. He was so full of regret that he had to give up his lodging at the Moor's and stay in a hotel instead. He had said, "If old man Moor had been alive such a thing would never have happened. It's the old lady who has messed it all up."'

When Notubiharibabu got off at Betol station and the train began to move, Jaganmaybabu noticed, near the platform, behind the iron railing, the same flowering bush. Not just one or two. Strewn all over a field—at least a hundred of them.

And in that field could be seen three baby goats playing with each other in sheer bliss.

4

The McKenzie Fruit[*]

I

Nishikantababu discovered the amazing tree in McKenzie Sahib's garden. He had heard about the sahib's attachment to trees and plants soon after his arrival in Karimganj. Within seven years of India's independence, the sahib had returned to his own country in Australia, and the bungalow had remained vacant ever since. People say the sahib's wife had been struck dead by lightning in this very house, and on full-moon nights an apparition clad in white could be seen roaming the garden. Because of this, no one went anywhere near the house.

After retiring as a teacher from Baharampur Government School, Nishikantababu had come to Karimganj to get treatment for his arthritis from Madhav Kabiraj. Madhav

---

* First published in *Sandesh*, 1981

Kabiraj might not have had a countrywide reputation, but he was certainly well known locally. It had been decided that Nishikantababu would stay at his friend Tarak Bagchi's house during the course of his treatment and then return home. But that was not to be. To begin with, soon after his arrival, Nishikantababu had been informed of Madhav Kabiraj's demise one-and-a-half months ago. Then, Tarak Bagchi had said, 'You're a bachelor. Who will you return to in Baharampur? Stay here. The climate of Karimganj will cure your arthritis.'

Nishikantababu could not turn down this request. Only once did he return to Baharampur to pack up his belongings. Ever since, he had been staying with his friend as a paying guest. Tarakbabu had built a tidy house in 1964 from his earnings as a munsif. He had lost his wife three years ago, his daughter was married and his son worked in Dehradun.

Undoubtedly, Karimganj was a pleasant city. It had housed a silk factory once, which was also what had brought the McKenzies to settle here. The factory had been defunct for the last hundred years, yet the charm of the city hadn't allowed the McKenzies to leave. The last sahib, John McKenzie, would have stayed back too had the death of his wife not broken him. Thus, his son, who traded in silk, had invited him to settle in Australia.

There was one thing Nishikantababu and his friend did not have in common. While Tarakbabu was a homebound person, happy to relax in an easy chair after returning from work, Nishikantababu was a passionate walker. Despite his arthritis, he was compelled to walk at least two or three kilometres every evening.

Within three days of arriving in Karimganj, the McKenzies' abandoned bungalow caught Nishikantababu's attention. Bound by a fence, this picturesque building with a sloping tiled roof stood on two acres of land. It was flanked by verandahs in the front and back and surrounded by numerous trees.

Nishikantababu had always been very fond of plants. Botany had been his favourite subject in college and his house in Baharampur had a small patch of garden. In addition to this was his natural penchant for exploration, which made it impossible for him to resist exploring such a wide variety of trees. On 10 October 1980—the date is crucial—disobeying his friend's orders, Nishikantababu hitched up his dhoti to his knees and jumped over a broken-down portion of the fence to enter McKenzie Sahib's garden.

Apart from homegrown varieties like mango, jamun, jackfruit, guava and coconut, Nishikantababu also spotted samples of a few foreign trees he had seen in pictures as well as in Shibpur Botanical Gardens. Nothing was left of the flowering trees, and the garden was overgrown with weeds.

Nishikantababu, fully in the grip of his indomitable curiosity, continued to explore further. A stone-inlaid path cut through the garden in a zigzag pattern. Marble statues, iron benches and a dried-up fountain were laid out across the garden. The McKenzies were fancy people indeed.

As Nishikantababu approached the far end of the garden, he caught an unfamiliar smell. It was pleasant, fresh, perhaps a flower or a fruit. He picked up pace. It was autumn; the days were shorter and dusk was going to fall soon. He only had so much time to detect the source of the smell.

Nishikantababu walked past a lion's statue and came to a halt. In front of him, towards the left, was an oleander tree, right behind which in a somewhat open area was a tree swathed in the golden sheen of the setting sun. He had never before seen a tree like this.

Nishikantababu took one step towards it. There was no doubt that the smell belonged to this tree. To a fruit from this tree. A white fruit, which was round at the top and had a pointed tip at the other end. The width of the round portion was that of a medium-sized orange. As Nishikantababu examined the leaves, he recalled a few terms he had learnt in botany class. The colour of the leaf was dark green; it was a compound leaf, oblong and serrated. The tree was as tall as the average height of a human being and a half. There were at least fifty fruits hanging from it, and though the sunlight on them was slowly fading, the fruits were emanating their own glow, drawing attention even in the darkness.

After observing the tree from various angles, Nishikantababu finally emerged from his trance. There would be no dearth of creepy-crawlies in this neglected garden. It was time for him to leave. But should he go empty-handed? Of course not. He raised his hand,

plucked a fruit from the extraordinary tree and headed homewards.

Upon seeing the fruit, even Tarakbabu was intrigued, though not quite like Nishikantababu. 'Now what have you brought with you?'

After Nishikantababu's explanation, Tarakbabu took the fruit in his hands and examined it thoroughly. Then he shook his head and said, 'I've never come across something like this before. This has to be a fruit from Australia.'

'But how will I confirm it?' Nishikantababu couldn't relax. He had to find out the name of the fruit.

'Go, show it to Gyanbabu,' said Tarakbabu. 'He has travelled to many foreign lands. See if he can identify it.'

Gyanbabu aka Gyanprakash Choudhury, sixty-five years old. The Choudhurys were the zamindars of Karimganj. Gyanprakash had had wanderlust. In his youth, when zamindari had still been flourishing, he had used his father's money to travel far and wide. He had collected a wide range of souvenirs from different countries and had filled his house with them.

Following his friend's advice, Nishikantababu put the fruit inside a bag and went to meet Gyanbabu. The latter was sitting in his drawing room listening to music. His latest passions consisted of listening to old Bengali music and collecting stamps. The gentleman did not believe in a modern record player and was playing music on a wind-up gramophone with a big horn.

The record ran for three minutes, playing a song by Zohra Bai. After the song finished, Gyanbabu switched off the machine and asked Nishikantababu to take a seat. The latter took out the fruit from his bag and put it on the marble-top table. Then he sat down on the sofa. 'What's that?' Gyanbabu peered at the fruit.

In a gentle voice, Nishikantababu said, 'Sir, I've come all the way only for this. I found this fruit in McKenzie Sahib's garden, but am unable to identify it. Since you've travelled so much . . . I thought . . .'

'Show it to me.'

Nishikantababu handed over the fruit to him. After stroking it and smelling it at length, Gyan Choudhury shook his head. 'I don't know this fruit. I'd suggest you show it to a botanist. I think the botanist at Presidency College is one Vinay Som. I spotted his name in the papers the other day. See if he can shed some light on this.'

This left Nishikantababu in a quandary. Would he now have to travel with the fruit to Calcutta?

As if reading his mind, Gyanbabu said, 'One of my sons has a polaroid camera. He will take a colour photograph of the fruit and the tree. You can send that to Som, and then wait for his reply.'

Jyotiprakash Choudhury, one of Gyanbabu's three sons, was a Canada-based professor who happened to be in Karimganj, waiting to get married. He willingly took a photo of the unknown tree with his camera. Nishikantababu watched with amazement as a white card instantly slid out of the slit in the camera as soon as the shutter was pressed. And right before his eyes, like magic, the picture of the tree appeared on that card. Jyotiprakash tore out the card from the camera and gave it to Nishikantababu.

Nishikantababu hesitated as he took the photograph from him. 'Only one . . . suppose it gets misplaced . . .?'

Without further ado, Jyotiprakash produced two more photos of the tree.

Nishikantababu wrote a description of the tree based on his college-level knowledge and sent it to Professor Vinay Som along with a copy of the photograph. Within seven days he received a reply. Vinay Som had never seen a tree like this before.

But Nishikantababu wasn't about to give up. This time he sent another copy of the photo along with the description to England's Royal Botanical Society. He took the address from *Whitaker's Almanack* that he had seen in Gyanbabu's house. The response took three weeks.

On behalf of the society, Mr Mortimer stated that provided the image of the tree and its fruit had not been tampered with, one had to admit that the species of this tree was unknown.

What transpired next disclosed another side to Nishikantababu's personality, the ingenious one. Lying in his bed one night, he fell into deep contemplation. Humankind had been consuming a variety of vegetables, fruits and cereals as food, but when did this start? Mango, apple, banana, orange, papaya, guava—there's been no mention in history of when humans first ate these fruits. Who discovered that a certain fruit was delicious, or that a particular food was nutritious, and when? There are many items that are not suitable for human consumption and can cause severe damage. Some varieties of mushrooms can be fatal for humans.

The vices and virtues of various foods find a mention in the scriptures. But these scriptures were produced only recently, much later than the birth of the human civilization. Human beings had started consuming these foods millions of years ago. Was there any document in history saying that this particular fruit or cereal was consumed by this particular person for the first time today to prove that it was edible? To test whether certain items were unsuitable for human consumption, they had to be eaten!

Following this chain of thought, one day Nishikantababu decided that this new fruit—which he now called the McKenzie fruit—must be tasted. He didn't disclose this decision to his friend as he would either be indifferent or put a stop to it. Nishikantababu wanted neither to happen.

The very next day, on his morning walk, Nishikantababu headed straight to McKenzie Sahib's garden. He was a bit apprehensive that the tree might no longer have any fruit or all of it would have dropped to the ground. On the contrary, when he reached he saw that there were even more fruit on the tree now than the previous day. Nishikantababu chose three of the most succulent ones, put them inside the bag he had carried with him and headed homewards. He could feel his heart beating much faster than normal. What he was about to accomplish today hadn't been attempted by anyone in this world before.

Had it, though? The tree was in McKenzie Sahib's garden. Hadn't he ever tasted the fruit?

This thought sucked the joy out of him momentarily, just like a blotting paper soaking up ink. Who could provide an answer to this question? First, he had to find out if anyone in Karimganj had been close to McKenzie Sahib. And only then would he consume the fruit.

The answer came from Tarakbabu.

'McKenzie hadn't been too keen on mixing with people,' Tarakbabu said. 'But I noticed him meeting up with the lawyer Shivsaran a few times. They had perhaps come to know each other in connection with a court case.'

It was Shivsaran who finally enlightened Nishikantababu. 'It had nothing to do with any court case. He had been fond of gardening and so had I. And thanks to this we had come to know each other. My garden produces forty-three varieties of roses. McKenzie had been full of praise when he'd seen it.'

Encouraged by what Shivsaran told him, Nishikantababu took out the fruit from his bag. 'Did you ever notice this fruit in McKenzie Sahib's garden?'

Shivsaran knit his brow. 'This is from the sahib's garden?'

'Yes, sir.'

'Where exactly?'

Nishikantababu described the location of the tree.

'Is there an amla tree struck by lightning around that area?' Shivsaran asked.

Yes indeed, Nishikantababu recalled. The unknown tree was situated on the east side, a few metres from the burnt tree. 'This indicates the tree is located exactly where the memsahib had died,' said the lawyer. 'But during the sahib's time this tree hadn't existed. Had it been there, it would have caught my attention. Many a time I've walked around that garden with the sahib.'

Nishikantababu heaved a sigh of relief. Now there were no hurdles in his path towards becoming a pioneer. He would be the first to eat the fruit of the unknown tree.

That night, after a dinner of dry vegetables, masur dal and fish curry prepared by his cook Nitai, Nishikantababu sat with his friend in the east verandah chatting. Half an hour later, he retired to his room. Clouds had already appeared in the evening sky, and now at 10 p.m., heavy rain pelted down with lightning and thunder. After shutting the door, he poured water from the pitcher into a glass and put it on the bedside table. He then took a McKenzie fruit in his hand, paid his respect to the picture of the Paramhansa hanging on the wall in front of him, straightened up and bit into the fruit.

After three bites, when the juice of the fruit travelled through his food pipe, Nishikantababu realized that this was a sacred fruit. There could be no other like it. It was well beyond comparison. He took five minutes to finish the entire fruit. The time was a quarter to eleven. There was no question of getting any sleep now. He could feel a great excitement accompanied by a tinge of apprehension in his heart. If the fruit was going to have any adverse reaction, the signs would become visible tonight itself.

Throughout the night, Nishikantababu checked his pulse at frequent intervals. Every half an hour, he stood in front of the mirror on the wall to examine his face for any unpleasant changes. Finally, at midnight, he left his room and began to pace up and down the street to ascertain that all his muscles were working well.

After five o'clock, when the birds began to chirp, Nishikantababu noticed that his arthritis had completely disappeared, and that he had never felt better in the last thirty years.

II

It didn't seem fair to Nishikantababu to be the sole beneficiary of the amazing McKenzie fruit. Furthermore, he felt it important to disclose that he had been the first to find the fruit and taste it. Nishikantababu jolly well knew that his friend had not an iota of interest in the matter. When he thought about bringing the discovery to the notice of a bigwig in the city, the first person he thought of was Gyanbabu. Nishikantababu was aware that different people had different tastes in life. But he wasn't convinced that anyone could dislike this delectable fruit.

Thus, he took one fruit along with him as he left for the Choudhury residence.

Nishikantababu felt a bit dispirited when he saw a non-Bengali guest sitting in the drawing room with Gyanbabu. Yet, without much ado, he explained his presence, took out the fruit from his bag and placed it on the table in front of Gyanbabu.

'Could you figure out the name of this fruit?' Gyanbabu inquired.

Nishikantababu informed him that even the Royal Botanical Society hadn't been able to identify it. 'Why don't you try it? It's such a delicious fruit.'

Gyanbabu didn't object. Instead of biting into it, he asked his retainer to get him a knife and two plates. After cutting the fruit, Gyanbabu took one piece for himself and gave the other to his guest. Nishikantababu was filled with joy when he saw the look on their faces as they finished eating the fruit.

'This is so tasty, my friend!' exclaimed Gyanbabu.

'Wonderful!' said the other gentleman. 'Delicious! From where did you get this fruit?'

Nishikantababu, in all innocence, explained everything to them, including his recovery from arthritis.

'McKenzie fruit. Did you come up with this name?' the non-Bengali fellow queried.

'It had to have a name,' Nishikantababu said. 'I couldn't think of anything else.'

Both gentlemen admitted that the name sounded grand.

Nishikantababu stepped out of the Choudhury residence feeling very pleased with himself. He was going to leave his mark on the world. Could anyone have foreseen that this sixty-two-year-old man leading such a mundane life would accomplish such a feat? No, they couldn't have. An ordinary man with an ordinary lifestyle, no different from millions of other mediocre people. But today, he was distinct. Not just among Bengalis or Indians, but the entire world.

But this was not the finale to his exploit. Only by bringing the fruit to all people could he really take credit for it. Nishikantababu's chest widened with pride. An extensive cultivation of the fruit would bring benefits to one and all. He had retained the seed of the fruit—a tiny black seed inside a light mauve pulp. Wouldn't it grow into a tree once it was planted in the soil? There was a patch of land behind his house, next to the gourd scaffold. Was there any harm in trying it out?

But it was not to be. Planting the seed in the soil yielded no result. Even after waiting for a week it showed no signs of sprouting.

Meanwhile, Nishikantababu discovered many other beneficial properties of the fruit. Abani Ghosh's eight-year-old son Bhuto came to his house to take math lessons. After eating the fruit, he was cured of his pharyngitis. A wounded dog in the neighbourhood was often seen hanging around in the front verandah of Tarakbabu's house. A few days after he had given it a piece of the fruit, Nishikantababu noticed that its sore had healed. Unbeknownst to Tarakbabu, Nishikantababu mixed a spoon of the fruit's juice even in his friend's tea, which cured the latter's ten-day-old chest congestion overnight.

Would it be fair for only the locals of Karimganj to know about this fruit? Would it never travel beyond the city? Nishikantababu still had one photo of the fruit taken by Jyotiprakash with him. He wrote an article about the fruit on four foolscap sheets, and along with the photograph sent it to *The Statesman*. He called the article, 'A Wonderful New Fruit'. Needless to add, Nishikantababu made it clear that he alone was responsible for discovering this fruit. In such a scenario it was not easy to stay away from self-promotion, was it?

After seven days, a twenty-five-year-old lad came to meet Nishikantababu at home. He was Anjan Sengupta, a reporter from *The Statesman*. His appearance was smart, he wore a pair of thick glasses, and had a camera and tape recorder with him. He had been sent to collect more information about the fruit.

Nishikantababu looked quite pleased. What could be nicer? This was exactly what he was expecting.

'Hope you'll be carrying my article?' Nishikantababu asked.

'Well, nowadays people prefer an interview rather than an article,' said Anjan Sengupta. 'Um . . . is there any way I could get to see that tree?'

'Of course, you can,' said Nishikantababu, 'but we'll have to walk a couple of kilometres.'

They headed out in the direction of McKenzie Sahib's garden. Nishikantababu hadn't visited the garden in ten days. On his last visit he had seen the tree almost drooping with the weight of so many fruits. Did that mean this was a tree for all seasons? Would it bear fruits all through the year? Many such thoughts crossed his mind as they made their way to the garden.

But how strange! In the last few months no one had entered this garden other than him—except Jyotiprakash with his camera—but why was there a motley crowd today?

Nishikantababu identified two individuals in the crowd—Gyanprakash Choudhury and that non-Bengali friend of his. Today Gyanbabu introduced him.

'You saw him that day. This is Chunilal Mansukhani. Ever since he tasted your fruit, his head has been buzzing with ideas.'

'Really?' For no apparent reason, Nishikantababu's heart started hammering in his chest. He could gather that some kind of action was about to unfold.

'Mr Mansukhani desires to cultivate this fruit. He's a businessman after all, and once he senses an opportunity, no way can you stop him.'

Nishikantababu felt the need to speak up. 'But I've tried planting seeds. There were no signs of any sapling.'

Mansukhani chuckled. 'The tree grows only in this soil. See how saplings have started appearing from seeds sown a week ago.'

Nishikantababu was surprised to see that a few yards from the tree, on the right, a fresh new sapling had appeared; he could easily identify the leaves.

The journalist, sniffing a bigger and better story, dropped Nishikantababu and interviewed Mansukhani instead. As a result, in place of Nishikantababu's article, Mansukhani's interview appeared in the paper.

In six months' time, McKenzie Sahib's garden was completely covered with the tree. In a month's time, Gyan Choudhury and Mansukhani struck a partnership deal and their business took off. There were only a hundred and sixty-two trees in the garden, but they bore fruit throughout the year. In the meantime, a laboratory test of the fruit showed it had seven types of vitamins. Some other elements were also noted, which chemists were yet to identify.

Its flavour, usefulness and limited availability resulted in the fruit being sold at sky-high rates. Each tin consisted of peeled slices of four deseeded fruits cut into two pieces, packed in a sugary syrup with preservatives. At the Indian rate, each tin was priced at Rs 350. People of this country had to content themselves with only the news of the fruit as it was being exported to Japan, Europe and America, and would never reach their homes. The reputation of the fruit spread across the world like wildfire, yet, despite several attempts, it remained impossible to grow the fruit anywhere except in McKenzie Sahib's garden.

In the garden as well as in Birsinghapur, which was close to Karimganj and housed the tin factory, a strong police presence was established. On all sides of the garden, strong walls were erected, which reminded one of a prison. The bungalow was demolished and a brand-new office was built for the McKenzie Fruit Company. Every day at 9 a.m., Mansukhani arrived in the office in his Mercedes. A few close associates and friends too would visit the office occasionally and leave with tins of the fruit bought at concessional rates. Other than the official workers no one was allowed to enter the premises.

One-and-a-half years went by. Nishikantababu was yet to come out of his utterly baffled state. He had gone to see McKenzie Sahib's garden two days after the opening of the office, but the police had not allowed him to enter. Completely taken aback he had tried to explain in Hindi, 'I'm Nishikanta Bose. I discovered this fruit. Go tell your bosses this.' But the armed guard at the door had paid no heed to his words. It had been no different when he had gone to meet Gyanbabu at his house as he no longer met with commoners.

Of course, by now all this information had reached Tarakbabu's ears. In a voice oozing with scorn, he told his friend, 'You have a lawyer friend. Yet, without consulting him, you took hasty decisions all on your own. How will you understand the mindset of these unscrupulous people? Seeing your gullibility, it's no surprise that they outwitted you.'

All said and done, Nishikantababu still had one fruit left with him. After much trouble he managed to obtain an empty tin from the Birsinghapur factory and put the fruit inside it. This fruit was his discovery. It was he who had first tasted it and he who had given it its name, McKenzie fruit.

And even after one-and-a-half years, this amazing fruit was still intact.

5

The First-Class Compartment[*]

The first-class train compartment—the four- or six-berth coach with a bathroom—no longer exists. But in 1970, the year in which this story is set, such compartments, though rare, were still around. Those fortunate travellers who were used to old coaches would think they had reached the moon if they found themselves in one of these compartments.

This is exactly how Ranjanbabu felt when he boarded the train. At first, he couldn't believe his luck. He couldn't recollect when he had last been on a journey in a coach like this. Being the son of a wealthy father, even as a child he had been quite used to travelling first class. When the single compartment had been replaced by the six-compartment special corridor train, Ranjanbabu had felt a comfort from his life as well as the country disappear.

---

* First published in *Sandesh*, 1982

He had observed many such changes in the last few years. His father had owned a Buick. How much Ranjanbabu had enjoyed those joyrides, reclining on the back seat with his legs outstretched. Then had come the time of Fiat-Ambassador, bringing an end to another comfort. During the British era, each time you picked up the phone, a female voice would say, 'Number please,' and after you had given the number, you would be connected immediately. And now, your fingers turned stiff as you dialled the number again and again. It was as if the idea of luxury was rapidly evaporating from the city. Ranjanbabu had never needed to travel by bus or a tram, but was there any joy even travelling in a car any more? Those relentless jams were suffocating. And count your blessings if you hit a pothole and your bones didn't break!

In Ranjanbabu's view this was the net result of India's independence. It had never been like this during the Raj. Calcutta in those days had indeed been a civilized city of a civilized state.

Three years ago, Ranjanbabu had spent six months in London. The English knew how to live, knew the real value of a disciplined life, and they truly appreciated civic sense. One couldn't help but be deeply impressed by their Tube that worked with clockwork precision. It was as populated as Calcutta, yet there had been no rush at bus stops, no shouting or screaming by conductors or banging against the bus. The buses hadn't tilted so much as to make one think that they might overturn at any moment.

In his circle of friends, Ranjanbabu's fascination for the Brits had always been the main subject of discussion. Of course, the tone had been more of ridicule and Ranjanbabu had lost many friends. In a city where there were hardly any English, how could one endure this constant praise of them and their era? Pulakesh Sarkar, his childhood friend, had continued to be his friend, but even he, given a chance, couldn't stop himself from deriding Ranjanbabu. He would say, 'It's such a grave mistake that you were born in this country. Your national anthem ought to be "God Save the Queen" and not "Jana Gana Mana". You won't survive for long in this independent, "native" country.'

This wouldn't stop Ranjanbabu from scornfully replying, 'It's a sign of narrow-mindedness if you don't admire and accept their virtues. The Bengalis boast about their Calcutta, but the real beauty of Calcutta, the Maidan, was made by the English. Anything of splendour is their creation. You can't call Bagbajar, Shyambajar and Bhawanipore spots of beauty. Moreover, these attractive locales will not remain so for long, and these native Bengalis will be responsible.'

These two friends had gone to Raipur in Madhya Pradesh on a holiday. Ranjan Kundu held a high post in an international corporate office, and Pulakesh was the manager of a noted advertising company. This year Puja and Eid had amounted to ten days of holidays. Their plan had been to spend a week with their common friend Mohit Bose, take car rides to the forest areas of Bastar, and then return to Calcutta together. Pulakesh had mentioned that he planned to spend a couple of days with his cousin in Bhilai but Ranjanbabu hadn't allowed it. He had said, 'We have come together and we shall return together. I just don't like travelling alone, my friend.'

However, even after arriving at the station, Pulakesh had had to stay back. Bhilai was about ten miles from Raipur, and Pulakesh's cousin had landed up at the station to take Pulakesh back with him. The Bengalis of Bhilai had decided to organize Tagore's play *Bisarjan* during Puja. Since Pulakesh was passionate about theatre, his cousin had been keen to have him direct the play. Pulakesh couldn't refuse.

Ranjanbabu would've been upset, but when he saw the old first-class compartment, he didn't feel the impending absence of his friend that severely. It was even more delightful that despite belonging to a bygone era, the coach was neat and tidy. All the bulbs worked, fans moved, and there were no tears on the leather seats. The bathroom too was clean and fresh.

Moreover, there were no other passengers in these four berths apart from Ranjan Kundu and Pulakesh Sarkar. Pulakesh informed him, 'You can travel alone till Rourkela. Only one passenger will join you. The two upper berths will remain empty during the rest of your journey.'

Ranjanbabu remarked, 'So many times I've regaled you with the comforts of such a coach. The regret is, despite getting this chance, you can't take up the offer.'

The friend smiled and said, 'A fellow from Kellner will arrive to take your dinner order.'

'Now don't you upset me. Nowadays I find train food almost revolting. In our childhood, how much we looked forward to lunch and dinner from Kellner.'

Ranjanbabu had of course got a packed lunch of puri and sabzi with him in a tiffin carrier from his friend's house. He was not at all keen on the train thali.

In due course the Bombay Mail began moving. 'I'll meet you in Calcutta, dear friend,' said Pulakesh. 'Undoubtedly your journey will be quite comfortable.'

A few minutes after the train left the station, Ranjanbabu started pacing the compartment. He hadn't experienced this kind of luxury in a long time. In the coaches of today one had no choice but to settle down in one's seat the moment the train started moving. The corridor outside was so narrow that one couldn't even take a walk. Only at a station could you walk on the platform. For the rest of the journey, you had to remain seated, almost motionless.

After that brief walk, pondering over which seat to occupy, he finally decided on the one facing the Raipur platform. He sat down, opened his suitcase, took out a pillow and a detective novel and lay down. It was now 5.30 in the evening, and it would get dark in no time. But that wouldn't prevent him from reading as there was a lamp on the wall behind him and it worked.

When the train left Raigunge at 9 p.m., Ranjanbabu felt a bit drowsy. The staff had come to take his dinner order in Bilaspur. Unsurprisingly, Ranjanbabu had declined the offer. He now opened his tiffin carrier, finished his repast, switched off all the lights except the blue one and finally lay down. Just then he remembered that the other passenger would come into his coach in Rourkela. Nowadays in the corridor trains, when passengers arrived in the first-class compartment, the conductor would usher them in. In this old coach, he would have to open the door himself. Should he lock the door? What if he didn't wake up? Would it be okay if he didn't lock it? Whoever came could lock it themselves. In any case it wouldn't be that late in the night. The train would reach Rourkela at 10.30 p.m. There was no need to worry.

The Bombay Mail was chugging along at great speed. Some found the rocking motion difficult to sleep in but Ranjanbabu had no such problem. He had read that after a child grows up it can still retain the memory of its mother rocking it to sleep in her lap. Therefore, feeling sleepy from the train's movement was nothing unusual. Ruminating on his childhood memory of relishing Kellner's chicken curry with rice and custard pudding, Ranjanbabu slipped into deep slumber.

'Hot tea! Hot tea!'

Ranjanbabu woke as the vendor's cry came from outside the window. Station. The light from the lamppost on the platform fell partially on him and partly on the floor of his room.

'Hindu tea! Hindu tea!'*

The eternal cry of a station hawker. It was as if the same person had been shouting ceaselessly in all the stations across India. Ranjanbabu peered out from the window but couldn't spot the name of the station. Could this be Rourkela?

The moment he remembered this, his eyes shifted towards the opposite bench. He had heard the sound of bells when he had woken up. In the hazy blue light, he could see a figure sitting across him, with two bottles and a glass resting in front of him. The passenger had just poured some liquid in the glass, and was now bringing it towards his mouth.

---

* 'The cry of "Chai! Guram gurram chai" (tea, hot tea!) mingled with the shouts of *pani* carriers calling out "Hindu Pani!", "Muslim Pani!" Muslim rail passengers were less bothered by the caste restrictions that hindered Hindus from accepting food or even water from anyone of a lower caste, and they took to tea with enthusiasm. Though the European instructors took great care to guide the tea vendors in the correct way of making a cup of tea, they often ignored this advice and made tea their own way with plenty of milk and lots of sugar . . .' (Extract from *Curry: A Tale of Cooks and Conquerors* by Lizzie Collingham; 2006)

Was he drinking? Had he boarded the train in Rourkela? Was this station then Chakradharpur? It did seem like quite a big station.

Ranjanbabu looked straight at the stranger. His face wasn't very clear but Ranjanbabu gathered that he was sporting a thick moustache. He was attired in a shirt and trousers, though their colours weren't clear in the darkness.

As Ranjanbabu shifted, the stranger became alert. Ranjanbabu got a whiff of alcohol. He did not have this evil habit himself, yet he knew others who drank. Because of the various parties he had attended, he had become adept at identifying the smell of different drinks. So he knew the stranger was drinking whisky.

'You there,' the stranger roared at Ranjanbabu in a hoarse voice.

Ranjanbabu gathered from both the voice and the accent that he was none other than an Englishman. The timbre of his voice was extraordinary.

'You there,' the man rumbled at Ranjanbabu again. He must already be quite inebriated, otherwise why would he be so ill-tempered?

'Are you trying to tell me something?' Ranjanbabu asked in English. This sahib was such a fitting traveller in this old coach, he thought.

'Yes,' said the sahib. 'Get out and leave me alone.'

Ranjanbabu realized that this gentleman was indeed very drunk. But he ought to give him a proper response.

In a measured tone, he said, 'I too have a reservation in this coach. We both can stay here together. There's no harm in that, is there?'

Just then, the train sounded its horn following the guard's whistle, and with a jerk they resumed their journey. Ranjanbabu quickly checked the name of the station—it was indeed Chakradharpur.

There was no light in the compartment apart from the blue light. In order to see the sahib more clearly or rather to reassure himself, Ranjanbabu stretched his hand towards the light switch.

'Don't!' the sahib barked.

Ranjanbabu pulled his hand back. But that was all right. He had got used to the darkness and could see the sahib's face more clearly now. The first thing he noticed again was his moustache. His eyes were deep-set, and in the reflection of the blue light his skin looked rather pale. Ranjanbabu couldn't figure out if his hair was golden or white.

'I can't possibly travel with a nigger. Like I said, please get off.'

Nigger. Ranjanbabu couldn't imagine any sahib having the courage to say that to an Indian in the India of 1970. He had heard of similar incidents during the British time, not that he had ever been convinced of them. The Bengalis had often wrongly cast aspersions on the Brits. Even if these stories were true, those English must have belonged to a very low strata. Sahibs who were sober and civilized would never misbehave like this with an Indian.

Ranjanbabu had come out of the initial shock but was still trying to be patient. You couldn't afford to be impatient with a drunkard. In a sober state, this sahib would never have misbehaved like this.

Calmly, Ranjanbabu said, 'No one talks in that tone any more. I hope you know India has been an independent country for twenty-five years.'

'What?' the sahib exclaimed and burst into a loud guffaw, beating even the sound of the train.

'What did you say? India has gained independence? Since when?'

'In 1947. The fifteenth of August.'

Ranjanbabu suppressed a smile. To inform someone of our independence in our own country after twenty-five years was comical indeed.

'You must be mad.'

'I'm not mad, Sahib,' said Ranjanbabu. 'I think you're inebriated at the moment.'

'Is that so?'

Suddenly, the sahib picked up something from the right side of his bench. Fearfully Ranjanbabu noticed it was a revolver. And it was aimed straight at him.

'See this?' said the sahib. 'I'm an army man. My name is Major Davenport from the Second Punjab Regiment. No one has a sharper aim than me in my regiment. Is my

hand trembling? I'm aiming at the right of the third button of your shirt. If I press the trigger, the bullet will enter it and go out of the window. Nothing will be left of you. For your own safety, get out. As it is you're a nigger. On top of that you're insane. Do you know which year this is? It's 1932. That loinclothed leader of yours has given us enough trouble. You can always dream of your independence, but alas that will never see the light of day.'

Now the sahib had really turned delirious. It was 1970, not 1932! It had been twenty-three years since even our loinclothed Gandhiji had died.

'Come on now. Get up,' said the sahib, standing up.

Ranjanbabu's legs felt like they were made of rubber. Why was he speaking such rubbish? Was he actually insane?

'Up! Up!'

Ranjanbabu's throat was dry. Faced with no other choice, he stood. Without his knowledge, his hands went up.

'Now turn around and go to the door.'

What was he saying? The train was going at more than sixty kilometres per hour. Did he intend to throw Ranjanbabu out from a moving train?

Even under these trying circumstances Ranjanbabu managed to speak. 'Just listen to me, Major Davenport. Tatanagar station comes right after this. When the train stops, I promise I'll go to the next compartment. What's the point of throwing me out of a moving train and killing me?'

'Tatanagar? There's no station by that name. Once again you're talking nonsense.'

Ranjanbabu realized if the sahib was really convinced it was 1932, there would be no Tatanagar station.

Not considering it wise to argue, he simply said, 'That's fine, Major Davenport, it's my mistake. When the train stops at the next station, whichever that might be, I'll get off. You need not suffer a nigger beyond a couple of hours, I promise.'

The sahib relented somewhat and said, 'Make sure you do that. I assure you if you change your mind, your body will be found on the tracks.'

The sahib went back to his bench and put his revolver to one side. Ranjanbabu came back to his own seat, relieved he was still alive. Whatever the sahib might've said, Ranjanbabu was sure the next station was Tatanagar. It would take another hour to get there. Till then he would remain in this compartment. He didn't know what would happen after that. Would he get a seat in another first-class coach? He had no idea. And there was no way he could find out either.

Davenport Sahib was drinking once again. He seemed to have forgotten all about his co-passenger for the moment. Ranjanbabu kept his eyes half shut and stared at him. Who knew he would have to encounter such a dangerous situation? Had Pulakesh been here, would such an episode have taken place? No, Ranjanbabu didn't think so. But something much more serious could have occurred. Pulakesh was headstrong and physically powerful too. On top of that, he was fiercely patriotic and not the type to stomach such humiliation from a white-skinned person.

He would have perhaps hit the sahib. He still liked to regale his friends with how in his college days he had once punched a gora and broken his nose.

The train was piercing through the dark night. After ten minutes, Ranjanbabu realized he had dozed off with the rocking motion of the train, despite this perilous scenario. Then, a completely new thought struck him.

The sahib wasn't carrying any luggage with him. Not even hand luggage. Wasn't that a bit strange? Could anyone step into a train simply with a bottle each of alcohol and soda, a glass and a revolver? This being the year 1932, loinclothed leader, no Tatanagar—what did all of this indicate?

Could it mean that this sahib was not a real sahib but an apparition? Did the name Major Davenport ring a bell? Suddenly, Ranjanbabu recalled something.

About five years ago, there had been a discussion in his house with his barrister friend, Nikhil Sen, which had been chiefly focused on the adulation as well as derision of the English. Ranjanbabu couldn't remember who had said this but a gora soldier had once tried to remove a Bengali from the first-class coach of the Bombay Mail. His name had indeed been Major Davenport. It had been reported in the newspapers. The year was not known but it wouldn't be a surprise if it had been 1932. However, the sahib had miscalculated. That Bengali had been extremely courageous and had extraordinary strength. Not tolerating the humiliation, he had punched the sahib hard, who had fallen and hit his head against the bench, leading to his instant death.

Ranjanbabu felt a chill spread all over his body. Regardless, he couldn't help look at the fellow across from him once more. Major Davenport sat with a glass in his hand. The night light was not very bright. In addition to this was the rocking motion of the train. Altogether, the figure of the sahib appeared blurred. Perhaps he had died in this very coach in 1932. And ever since, every night in this old-fashioned, first-class coach . . .

Ranjanbabu couldn't think straight. The sahib was no longer looking in his direction. He was absorbed in his own drink. Staring at him, Ranjanbabu felt his eyelids getting heavier. That one could turn soporific in front of a ghost was something he was discovering for the first time. Major Davenport was there sometimes and would fade at other times. That is, when Ranjanbabu closed his eyes, the major would disappear and when he opened them, he would reappear. It's possible the sahib glanced at him one time. After that he heard a few words coming from afar—'dirty nigger . . . dirty nigger . . .'

Ranjanbabu didn't remember anything after this.

When he woke up, the early morning light appeared in the window. There was no one on the bench opposite him. He shuddered when he remembered the previous night's ordeal, but immediately afterwards, heaved a sigh of relief as he realized he was no longer in danger. There was no way he could narrate this story to anyone. To start with, no one would believe him. Also, it wouldn't be a matter of great pride to share the harassment he had suffered at the hands of an Englishman. Dirty nigger. These words had specifically hurt his vanity as he was rather fair-skinned. He was much fairer than the tan-skinned sahibs. Quite a few in London hadn't believed he was Indian. Yet the phrase, dirty nigger, had been flung at him of all people.

So, he didn't disclose his experience in the train to a soul. However, his near and dear ones noticed that there had been a definite change in his adulation of the English.

Ten years after the event, drinking coffee with Pulakesh in his house one evening, Ranjanbabu couldn't help but talk about the incident.

'Do you remember that day of our return from Raipur in 1970?'

'Of course!'

'I somehow couldn't tell you before, but you've no idea how I was hectored at the hands of a sahib apparition.'

'Was that Major Davenport's ghost?'

Ranjanbabu's eyes popped out. 'How do you know about that?'

Pulakesh stretched his right hand towards Ranjanbabu. 'Meet the ghost of Major Davenport.'

Ranjanbabu's head reeled. 'You! And all these days . . .?'

'If I'd told you, the entire mission would have failed. My aim was simple. I wanted you to get rid of your fawning over the English. If you weren't convinced, how could one have achieved that? Isn't there a difference between my saying "nigger" and a sahib saying "nigger"?'

'But how did you . . .?'

'Very easy,' said Pulakesh. 'The idea struck me the instant I saw your coach. After the train left, I hopped into the first-class bogey next to you. I used cotton from my first aid box to make that pair of moustache. Otherwise, there was no make-up. In my own coach, I saw a Gujarati boy carrying a toy revolver. He willingly gave it to me when I asked if I could borrow it. His father had whisky; I asked for that too. Of course, I had to explain all this to them. I only drank water and kept the whisky bottle open so that you could smell it. The rest was accomplished by that blue light, coupled with your own imagination. Hope you didn't mind, my friend.'

Ranjanbabu pressed his friend's hands warmly, but couldn't say a word. He would need another ten years to get over the shock.

6

A Hoax[*]

'How many volumes of Charles Wakeman's *History of Magic* do you possess?'

After signing the reply to a letter from the International Magic Circle, Samaresh Brohmo raised his head and looked at Mahim, who was his academic friend Ranen Sengupta's son. He had recently completed a librarianship course and had willingly taken upon himself the responsibility of arranging Uncle Samaresh's two thousand five hundred books thematically, as well as prepare a catalogue of his entire collection.

'Two volumes. Why?' said Samaresh.

'I can see only one. Where's the other?'

'Have you checked thoroughly?'

'Yes.'

---

* First published in *Sandesh*, 1982.

That was odd! The volume had now lost its partner in the set. Not even all the money in the world could procure a replacement copy any more.

Samaresh Brohmo's passion for books went back twenty-five years, to his college days. Though he had been a student of history, he had had a wide range of interests in books. He had books on travel, hunting, archaeology, anatomy. And magic. At first, magic had been a hobby for Samaresh, which had eventually turned into an addiction. His father, Adinath Brohmo, had been a noted barrister, who had been keen to have his son study law abroad. Samaresh had tried to do so by pursuing a course at the Trinity College in Cambridge, but within three months, he had come in contact with Marca Silverstone and his studies had gone to the dogs. Samaresh had informed his father that he would no longer continue to study law; instead, he desired to become a magician. To underscore his request, he even included a letter from Silverstone along with his own inside the envelope. Silverstone had written: 'I'm writing to you essentially as your son's friend—Samaresh is wonderfully clever with his hands. I see an assured future for him as a magician.'

Any other father, under such circumstances, would have either been anguished or enraged. But Adinath had been an exception. He had replied to his son, 'I've no wish to interfere in your independence. If you indeed possess any special skill, I'd certainly want you to master it.

If there's an opportunity to study magic in London, please don't hesitate to let me know the cost. I shall send you the amount.'

However, Samaresh hadn't stayed back in London. After two months, he had returned and begun to practise magic at home. He had been twenty-two then. At twenty-five, he had given his first public performance as a magician. This had, of course, been a solo show, focusing only on sleight of hand. All the same, critics had praised his dexterity highly in newspapers.

Along with his seven associates, including all the paraphernalia of stage illusions, Brohmo the Great had made his first public appearance at the age of thirty-two. Sitting in the front row, the standing ovation from the audience had made his father immensely proud.

Adinath died in 1974. As the only child, Samaresh inherited his entire property. But by then, his own income had been considerable. He had not only been getting invites from various parts of India, but had also started receiving offers from across the world. Samaresh was an excellent performer, and two tactics kept his audience spellbound. The act of narration is something magic show enthusiasts take for granted, yet Samaresh wouldn't open his mouth at all during his two-hour show. Instead, he would present his other unique offering. He had created an excellent raga-based orchestra comprising the sitar, sarod, flute and tabla, which played throughout his performance. This was a novel experience for each viewer. He would match a particular raga to go with a particular act and this would win everyone's heart.

By the age of forty-one, Samaresh had earned worldwide fame. His popularity kept pace with this progress. The moment his latest show was announced, tickets would be sold out within a week. Everyone, young and old, would emerge from the hall in a trance after witnessing his awe-inspiring performance. Samaresh too was well aware that his gift of bluffing an audience of more than two thousand was an art.

The Americans compared him with Thurston and Houdini; the British with Maskelyne and David Devanter; the French with Robert-Houdin; and the Chinese in Hong Kong with Ching Ling Foo. But this wasn't the end of his aspirations. He planned to keep surprising his audience with newer tricks and newer actions, and continue to astonish, marvel and amaze.

Therefore, his passion for buying books and reading never waned. Apart from books on regular magic, there were those on ancient magic like witchcraft, voodooism as well as hypnotism, clairvoyance, ventriloquism and so on, filling three large bookcases. He had also ordered ten to fifteen books recently published abroad. As he spent a lot of his time away from home, these books remained in a mess. Hence, he hadn't objected to his friend's son's suggestion. Mahim needed four more days to finish his work.

There had been a time when Samaresh had lent his books to his friends, though not necessarily of his own free will. He had never been able to say no to anyone, despite considering it a weakness. He had organized a register to record the titles of books against the names of those who had borrowed them, along with the lending date. When a book would be returned, Samaresh would strike off the person's name, add the date of return and sign on it.

With success one acquires a personality, and with it confidence. Perhaps due to this, in the last ten years, he had finally managed to put a stop to the lending of his books. He had been at ease telling people, 'Please pardon me, this is a request I can't accede to any more.' As everyone was now aware of this, people no longer asked him to lend books. So how could a book go missing?

Shouldn't one go through that register now? But who would've borrowed a book on magic—?

Yes, it was plausible! There was one such individual, Samaresh now remembered. He turned to Mahim, standing beside him.

'Mahim, on the right of my history bookshelf, there's a writing table. Have you seen it? There's a blue notebook inside its drawer. There was a time when I used to lend books, and whoever took books wrote it down in that notebook. Just check if anyone has borrowed *History of Magic.*'

Within a minute, Mahim brought the notebook back, his face lit up with a smile.

'Found it,' said Mahim. 'Last entry. The name hasn't been struck off.'

'Is it Sushil Talukdar?'

'Yes.'

'Thought as much! Let me have a look.'

Good. At least the book could be traced. Charles Wakeman's *History of Magic*, Volume I, had been borrowed by Sushil Talukdar on 10 October 1972. About ten years ago. Never returned. There was no doubt the signature was Sushil's.

But Sushil had come five days ago, in the evening. He had sent a note through Mahim wishing to see Samaresh. The latter had excused himself from meeting him by pretending to be unwell. He knew why Sushil wanted to meet him. He would've either made a plea to get a ticket to one of Samaresh's performances or would've begged Samaresh to mark his presence at a certain function. There had been a time when he had indeed performed in a local playground. But people forget that this Samaresh was no longer the Samaresh of the past. And the idea of wheedling out a ticket was such a typically Bengali syndrome. Tickets for football; tickets for cricket; tickets for theatre; tickets for concerts; tickets for a magic show—there was no end to the demand. The very idea of standing in a queue to buy a ticket was such a revolting notion for people. If they could get the ticket from the right person, why would they bother with the whole rigmarole? What a bunch of lazy folks. But Samaresh knew if he didn't comply, he would be instantly branded as vain. How could he disappoint old acquaintances?

'This gentleman had come the other day,' Mahim informed him.

'Yes. To ask for a favour, I bet. He could have easily brought the book along. But of course, he won't do so. At the time, the set had cost Rs 250. It has been out of print for ages. If it's reproduced now it's going to be priced at least Rs 1000.'

Pausing, Samaresh knitted his brows. Then he asked, 'What did he seem like? He studied with me in college. It's been ages since I met him.'

'He was thin with salt-and-pepper hair, bushy eyebrows and a sharp pair of eyes. I told him that you don't meet anyone at this time, yet he forced me to give you the note. He also said if you heard his name you may agree to meet him.'

'Hmm . . .'

Samaresh had totally forgotten that he had lent the book on magic to Sushil Talukdar. What a fool he had been ten years ago. How could anyone lend such a valuable book? That Sushil had a keen interest in magic was something Samaresh remembered. He had been quite adept at sleight-of-hand tricks. However, he had lacked both patience as well as perseverance.

In addition to that, he had never had a wealthy father like Samaresh. Thus, the idea of taking up magic as a profession had been out of the question for him. Yet, for the last ten years, this fellow had possessed one of the most valuable books on magic that had been taken from a set in Samaresh's collection.

The only glimmer of hope, now that it had been traced, was that there might be a way of getting it back.

That evening he had a show in Kalamandir. Around ten at night, the book crossed Samaresh's mind once again. Twelve years ago, he had shown it to Sushil right after purchasing the set. Sushil's comment too flashed through his mind—'One day, your name will be inscribed in the history of magic, Samaresh.'

Samaresh was aware that Sushil wasn't too well off. He had got married at a very young age, and had had two daughters thereafter. Samaresh had attended the annaprasan ceremony of one of them. He may have had some more children in the meantime. It was no surprise that he might be in need of money. What if he had sold the book? The mere thought of this priceless set being crippled wrenched Samaresh's heart. He was left with just one option. As Sushil had never returned the book himself, a letter needed to be sent to him as a reminder.

Samaresh wrote:

Dear Sushil,

You'd come that day but I couldn't meet you as I was indisposed. Hope you didn't mind. You had borrowed one of my books, the first volume of Wakeman's History of Magic, *on 10 October 1972. Your signature on the notebook indicates that. This book is part of my precious collection and has now been out of circulation for long. I will be very happy if you could return it to me as soon as possible. If you could come by in the morning you could then join me for tea.*

With best wishes,
Samaresh

After finishing the letter, Samaresh glanced over it a couple of times. He had been firm about returning the book without being too rude. The tone was just right.

After writing the address and sticking a stamp on the envelope, he handed it over to the driver, Raghunath, to be dropped off at the post office.

Granted, the Calcutta postal department was inefficient. Yet, even after giving them a leeway of five days for delivery, when there was still no sign of Sushil Talukdar, it annoyed Samaresh no end. What does one do now? Would it look too odd if he personally went and demanded his book back? Even if one assumed the letter never reached Sushil, and it got lost in the post, one wasn't left with any other choice.

Samaresh glanced at the bookshelf and noticed the empty space where the first volume should have been. It broke his heart. This was an example of real passion. He couldn't rest till he retrieved the book. Sushil Talukdar lived at 3/7 Madhav Lane. As the chance of finding him home on a Sunday morning was strong, Samaresh decided to call on him then. At 9 a.m., he pressed the doorbell. There were a reasonable number of people on the street now, and he thanked his stars that he wasn't a popular actor. No one could make out that he was Brohmo the Great. On stage he appeared in a French-cut beard and a moustache, and he had prohibited newspapers to publish his real likeness.

'Who are you looking for?' the retainer who opened the door asked.

'Is Sushilbabu home?'

'Yes, sir. What name should I announce?'

'Tell him Samareshbabu has come to see him.'

After offering Samaresh a seat, the retainer went inside to call his master.

Behind the door, Samaresh could see the drawing room with four chairs, a sofa and a Kashmiri centre table. On one side, atop a small bookcase, rested a radio covered with a cloth. On the wall hung three pictures, apart from two calendars.

Samaresh had to get up as soon as he had settled in a chair. Smiling, and eyes wide in surprise, his college friend appeared from behind a curtain.

'Oh dear! How fortunate am I! In which direction did the sun rise today?'

'You perhaps didn't receive my letter?'

'Of course I received it!'

'Then—?'

Samaresh looked flummoxed. Sushil sat on the chair opposite him.

'I know very well how compelling your passion for books is. The other day I noticed a considerable increase in your collection. I just thought if you didn't receive my reply, you would land up in my house. So my assumption worked, didn't it?'

Samaresh wasn't particularly comfortable about having to come to Sushil's house. He could gather quite well that their lives were now a world apart. Thanks to his magical skills, he had mesmerized millions of people in forty big cities spread across the world and would continue to do so in future. And Sushil? His world was so limited. The mere thought filled him with pity for the fellow. He would love to leave as soon he got his book back. He had no time to strike a conversation.

'You made the right move,' said Samaresh. 'Otherwise, I might not have come. I'm rather busy—there's a show already on in the city. If you could kindly return the book to me, I will take your leave.'

'Book?'

'You do have it, right?'

Sushil Talukdar let out a hearty laugh.

'I don't possess any book of yours, my friend.'

'What!' All of Samaresh's fears were confirmed. The book was gone.

'The book is in your own house,' said Sushil Talukdar.

'But how? I saw your own handwriting in the notebook—'

'Why not? I know where you keep the notebook. After talking to that young fellow, when I realized I couldn't meet you, I had an idea. I decided to pull your leg. The note I gave him for you was a pretext to make him go away. I then opened the drawer and found the notebook. I could see the magic book on the shelf. I wrote down the title of the book and my own name against it with a date ten years ago. Then I pulled out the first volume from the set and hid it in your own room.'

'Where?'

'That old gramophone of yours that resembles a box? If you open the lid, you'll find it there.'

'But . . . but . . .' Relief and bafflement pulled Samaresh in two different directions. 'What was the reason for this insane act?'

'The reason is a small one, my friend,' said Sushil Talukdar. 'That day I'd brought my daughters' autograph books with me. They were fascinated by your show and I'd told them that Brohmo the Great had been my batchmate in college. They pleaded with me for your autograph. But you chose not to meet me. They were very angry when they heard this and almost lost all respect for you. I knew this was expected, though not quite desirable. I told them that my poor friend couldn't meet me as he was unwell but now you'll see how he'll straightaway appear in our house. And that's exactly what happened. Come on, Runu, Jhunu. Come here and see just how right your father was!'

Soon, two slims girls, aged twelve and sixteen, appeared from behind the curtain. With demure smiles and excited looks they first paid respect to Samaresh and then offered their respective autograph books to him.

As Samaresh signed his name, he thought about how he had had no idea that there was a character in this very city of Calcutta who could play a hoax on him!

7

Worthless[*]

Worthless is a word that can so easily be applied to many people on many occasions. Take, for instance, our retainer Nobokeshto. 'Nobo, you're absolutely worthless.' I heard my mother utter this expression many a times in my childhood. But in reality, Nobo was a competent worker. His fondness for sleep was his only vice. Every afternoon, he would sleep beyond the stipulated time and be invariably late in putting the kettle to boil. Thus, instead of 4 p.m., tea would be served only by 4.30 p.m. And my mother would brand him with this epithet, more out of anger than anything else.

However, the word couldn't have been more apt for Shejokaka. I don't think anyone else deserved it as much. Shejokaka's proper name was Khsetramohan Sen and his nickname, Khetu. My father had four siblings. Baba was the

---

* First published in *Chokmoki*, 1984

eldest and then Mejo, Shejo, Shona and Chhoto. With the exception of Shejokaka, all others achieved great success in life. My father was a noted lawyer. Mejo was a reputed academic with a double master's in Sanskrit and history. Shona, as a successful businessman, built three houses for himself in Calcutta. Chhoto had earned accolades from well-reputed ustads in the field of Hindustani classical music. In addition, he received thirty-six gold and silver medals from wealthy connoisseurs of Hindustani music.

And Shejokaka? This story is about him, so it can't be told in just a few words.

An earthquake occurred when Shejokaka was born. People are of the view that this impacted his brain and therefore he ended up the way he did. As a matter of course, almost all infants suffer from measles and chickenpox. Shejokaka had both, in addition to whooping cough, diphtheria, dengue, eczema and smallpox. In infancy, he got hiccups seven times while crying, which turned his body blue and made him lose consciousness. At the age of seven, he began to stammer, which was cured at nine-and-a-half when he fell from a guava tree. He fractured his ankle as a result, and as Dr Biswas couldn't fix the bones properly, Shejokaka always walked with a limp. Owing to this, he couldn't participate in any sporting activities. An absence of hand-eye coordination made him incapable of playing carrom, and a lack of aptitude meant he couldn't play any card games either.

Like his other siblings, Shejokaka was admitted to school in due course. Yet, when he failed his FA examination three times in a row, his father—my grandfather—put a stop to his education. He said, 'Khetu, since you've turned out to be so worthless, spending so much money on your education is like throwing money down the drain. Yet you shouldn't live as a dependent. From today you'll accompany Bhombol to the market. Familiarize yourself with the types of fruits, vegetables, fish and meat. Soon you will take charge of shopping for the family.'

Uncle Bhombol was my father's distant cousin and was brought up and educated in this house. For quite some time, Shejokaka accompanied Uncle Bhombol to the market. And then one day, when people were coming to the house for dinner, my grandfather shoved two ten-rupee notes inside Shejokaka's kurta pocket and said, 'Let's see how competent you are. The responsibility of today's shopping rests with you.'

Alas, that was not to be. Shejokaka's pocket had a hole. The notes probably fell through even before he reached the market. How could anyone trust him after this?

My first memory of him is an evening during Diwali. I was three years old and he was thirty-three. In due course I'll disclose why I remember this incident. Shejokaka was crawling on the verandah, pretending to be a horse, while I was perched on his back as his rider. When a firework rocket from next door fell on the cot in the verandah, he instantly stood up in alarm. I was thrown off his back and landed on the cemented floor, leading to a head injury accompanied with profuse bleeding. For obvious reasons, Shejokaka was reviled by almost everyone in the household.

During my growing-up years, I kind of developed a sense of compassion towards him. Looking at his average height, average complexion and a face that reflected both joy and sorrow, I often wondered why everyone needed to be bright and efficient? Amidst so many people in the city, was there any harm in the existence of one Shejokaka?

Given a chance, I loved to catch up with him in the corner room on the first floor. After a few visits, I realized there was no point in asking him to tell me stories simply because he could never ever remember the end of any story.

'Then what happened, Shejokaka?'

'Then? Hmm . . . then . . . wait . . . then . . . then . . . then . . .'

His voice would turn feeble just like a harmonium running out of air. From storytelling, Shejokaka would turn to humming out of tune, and when he couldn't continue even that, he would nod off. I could gather that he had no energy or inclination to try and remember the end of the story. Leaving him in that state, I would tiptoe out of the room. And Shejokaka would never bother to call me back.

When I was about twelve years old, one day I went to his room and found him completely absorbed in a fat book. Upon asking, he said it was a book on Ayurveda.

'Why are you reading it, Shejokaka?' I asked.

Shejokaka thought for a moment, then replied in a grim tone, 'This too is an ailment, isn't it?'

'What is an ailment?'

'This problem of mine. Incapable of doing anything, can't easily recall everything, unable to comprehend very well—this must be a disease.'

What could I say? So I said, 'It must be, Shejokaka.'

'Then why wouldn't there be any treatment for this?'

'Are you thinking of self-treatment?'

I was aware that no one had ever thought of taking him for a consultation with a doctor. And frankly speaking, despite those numerous ailments he had suffered as a child, later in life he remained quite fit. His health was never quite an issue.

Shejokaka continued, 'I spotted this on a footpath in Chawk bazaar. Bought it for ten annas. It might be useful. I feel Ayurveda can treat even my kind of ailments.'

Two days later when I went to his room, I found him getting ready to go out. Canvas shoes on his feet, dhoti tucked in, a cotton shawl around his neck and an umbrella in his hand. It was monsoon season. He said, 'In Bhattacharya colony there's a tree behind that broken-down Shiv temple. I require its roots. Once I get them, I can relax.'

Shejokaka set off. The sky was getting darker. If it started raining, it would foil Shejokaka's plans.

After lingering for a few hours, I finally went back to my own room on the second floor. From the window to the south, I could clearly see the street in front. It didn't rain that day. As dusk settled, I saw Shejokaka returning. I raced down the stairs and met him at the main door.

'Did you get the roots?'

'No. I made a mistake. I should have carried a torch. The place was very wild and it was pitch-dark.'

'But what's this?'

While speaking with him, I'd noticed a red stain on his khadi kurta.

'Ah, yes. How come I didn't notice this?'

He took off his kurta to find a leech sticking to his chest. Just as Bhima had sucked Duryodhana's blood from his chest, this fellow too had puffed himself up with Shejokaka's blood. The moment I tapped the creature, it dropped to the floor.

But how could just a single leech cause so much damage to Shejokaka? In total, we found fourteen leeches on his shoulder, elbow, waist, calf, knee and ankle. He easily lost five to six ounces of blood that day. Needless to add, this episode put an end to his adventure with Ayurveda.

I was always a very bright student. During my time, FA entrance was replaced with matric. In the main examination at the university, I stood third and went to Calcutta to study science. Staying in a hostel, I completed my master's in physics, stood first and left for America. There, I earned an excellent reputation as a researcher. I began to teach in Chicago University, while continuing my research.

As I lived abroad, my connection with Shejokaka dwindled. I'd just started teaching when I received a piece of strange news in a letter from my mother. Apparently, Shejokaka had got a chance to act in a film. I must mention that Shejokaka's face faintly resembled Swami Vivekananda's. But his physique was not quite the same. Shejokaka was five feet six inches tall, yet everyone noticed the similarity in his eyes, nose and face with Vivekananda. When he got the news that a film was being made on the life of Ramakrishna Paramhansa that also featured Vivekananda, Shejokaka directly went to the producer and mentioned his desire to act in it. He had no difficulty getting the role.

However, after a couple of weeks, I learnt that he had been removed from the film. And why not? Despite shutting himself in his room and memorizing all his lines with utmost zeal, if in scene number one he blurted out the dialogue of scene number three in a reply to Ramakrishna, could it have worked? In other words, Shejokaka proved that he was worthless also as a film actor.

When I was forty-eight, my younger brother who was also in Chicago, told me in a letter that Shejokaka had become a disciple of a mendicant and had left for Coimbatore.

Last December, along with my wife and two daughters, I visited Calcutta to attend the wedding of my Chhotokaka's daughter. Born and brought up in that country, my daughters are completely American. In the meantime,

I hadn't heard anything about Shejokaka. Therefore, after arriving in Calcutta when I realized that he was living in the same city and was doing well, I naturally felt an urge to meet him. I was sixty at that time, and hence Shejokaka was ninety. I'd assumed he had passed on.

For the past three months he had been living with my aunt's son Dr Ranesh Gupta in his house in Fern Road. I also realized that religious convictions hadn't agreed with him. Even after ten years, idli-dosa held no appeal. Staying half-fed every day for those years had made him lose thirty kilos. When he heard I was in town he told his nephew doctor, 'Ask Jhontu to visit me.'

So one Sunday evening I landed up in Fern Road. In the candlelit room on the second floor, Calcutta undergoing one of its frequent bouts of load shedding, Shejokaka sat reclined against a bolster wrapped in a green muffler over a tussar covering.

One could certainly recognize him, but I must also add that he had preserved himself rather well. All his hair had indeed turned white, but more importantly, he had retained his hair. When he opened his mouth to grin widely at me, I noticed a dozen original teeth. And when he spoke, though his voice had become feeble, there was a touch of vigour in it. I had never observed this robustness in him before. Perhaps the realization that he was now the senior figure in the family and no longer needed to bow before anyone, had helped him acquire such a personality.

'Hello, dear Jhontu,' said Shejokaka. 'Tell me what you do in the US.'

I humbly explained the nature of my work to him.

'Physics? Research?' said Shejokaka. 'Do people revere you?'

My seventy-seven-year-old aunt, in a higher pitch than usual, brushed off my humility and informed him about my reputation.

'Is that so?' said Shejokaka. 'Have you won the Nobel Prize?'

I smiled gently and shook my head.

'Then what's the big deal? Tut, tut. Utterly worthless!' he said, reproachfully.

After being poked at with such scornful jibes, Shejokaka's verbal diarrhoea harassed me no end.

'At least you managed to escape to a different land. Here I thought coming to Calcutta would provide me relief and the last few days of my life would be spent in the presence of my near and dear ones. But what's happening in this city? Vultures have left nothing of it except a skeletal frame. There's no electricity for ten hours a day. Life is unbearable due to the bad air one inhales with every breath. The cost of everything is sky-high, so much so that I can't even satisfy my gluttonous stomach. Hell, hell, hell. Worthless, worthless.'

That day it dawned on me that my attachment to Shejokaka hadn't waned. How each of his wise words brought me such happiness. Perhaps we had been mistaken. We'd spent our lives misjudging him, but actually Shejokaka was a very sensible man and the rest of us on this earth were worthless.

However, Shejokaka proved this new realization wrong in a span of just a few days. One morning we received a call from my aunt's house to say that Shejokaka had left us in the early hours. And it wasn't just any day. My niece's wedding had been fixed for that evening in the sacred hours of the twilight.

8

Ramdhan's Flute[*]

The man looked familiar. Ramdhan peeped from behind a tree to take a closer look at him, and froze. Even after a gap of ten years it wasn't difficult to recognize Khageshbabu. Khagesh Khastagir, the man who rummaged through old bricks and stones.

Satyaprakashbabu of Bakultala was standing next to Khageshbabu. He said, 'But no one has cast any aspersions on this house. There are no ghosts or ghouls in its vicinity. You can easily spend two nights here. As you also have a retainer with you, there's no need to worry. You have been here before and have seen these beautiful temples. These are all a hundred and fifty to two hundred years old. People hardly ever come to our village. It's our great fortune that you are back here after such a long time.'

---

* Written in 1985, this was first published in *Aker Pithey Dui* (One upon Two) in 1988.

Khagesh Khastagir was Ramdhan's uncle's friend. He lived in Calcutta and practised archaeology or some such thing, for which he made trips to this village of Jamhati to study ancient terracotta temples. A few articles by him on his work had also occasionally appeared in newspapers.

Ramdhan was very curious about the nature of Khageshbabu's work, yet he could never summon up the courage to say so. Oh God, there was no way he could forget that one incident when he had dropped one of Khageshbabu's stone figurines. As it is the archaeologist was ill-tempered, and on top of that there had been this big loss. To punish Ramdhan, Khageshbabu had grabbed a clump of Ramdhan's hair in one hand and pulled up his narrow waist with the other. He had then lifted Ramdhan up over his head and flung him to the ground. Ramdhan had been in pain for ten days.

Ramdhan was essentially meek and mild in nature. When Khageshbabu had first come to their house, Ramdhan had been only seventeen. Everyone would repeatedly ask him to run errands for them and constantly shout at him. Drop the letter in the postbox—Ramdhan will do it; drop Bishu uncle at the station—let Ramdhan take him; it's a rainy day, get some savouries from Keshto's shop—Ramdhan will fetch them. As a result, Ramdhan had to be on his toes round the clock. If he slipped up, there would be no end to the reprimands. Starting with the host of the house to even his thirteen-year-old brother Bishtu, they had all rolled their eyes at him.

Satyaprakashbabu was overwhelmed when he realized that Khageshbabu had returned to their village after such a long gap and taken up a room in Ganguly's house. He said, 'From your work point of view, that south-facing room would be best, both in terms of light as well as air. You can see the Gonduki Mountain from there and work in complete peace and quiet.'

Oh dear! What a nuisance! Ramdhan's flute was still in that particular room. He was so attached to this special flute, which he had bought for four annas from a fair on the day of Rathyatra. They now had history together. These days, Ramdhan went to the north-facing field of his village, sat under a barren almond tree and played his flute. He spent a lot of his time doing that. He hardly ever stayed at home; mostly he wandered through various pastures all by himself. No one objected to this. It was for the better. They felt that since Ramdhan had served so many people on so many occasions, he was entitled to his freedom.

But what would happen to the flute now? This flute was of a different nature altogether. Over time, Ramdhan's playing had evolved so that no other flute could produce the same quality of sound. The only option now was to wait and watch. Once Khageshbabu left the house, he could quickly slip in and bring the flute out. There was no way he was going to risk coming come face-to-face with the archaeologist. He might still be nursing the anger from ten years ago! Ramdhan had noticed that Khageshbabu's face had hardly changed since then.

Khageshbabu arrived in the morning and did not budge from the room the whole afternoon. When the sun was about to set, Ramdhan, who was hiding behind the jackfruit tree, saw Khageshbabu stretch and step outside the front door. Would he finally go out? Ramdhan hid himself further behind the tree.

Khageshbabu went into the room once again, picked up his stick, and taking the road in front of the house, started walking eastwards. His manner suggested he was out for an evening walk. After waiting two minutes, Ramdhan emerged from behind the tree and proceeded towards the house. He also needed to avoid the servant, as the latter might end up raising an alarm if he mistook Ramdhan for a thief. Fortunately, the servant was inside the kitchen on the ground floor.

Using the stairs, Ramdhan headed straight towards the south-facing room on the first floor. The door was locked. He went around the verandah to try and enter from the window. That was only possible if the window had been kept open. Luckily, it had been.

Ramdhan climbed into the room from the window. A range of stone statuettes was strewn across a table.

Apart from these, there were papers, pens, pencils, pictures and an inkpot. But no flute. It had been in the alcove on the wall, but now all that was there was a lantern.

Clouds rumbled outside. Ramdhan had already seen black clouds gathering in the south-west. And now they seemed to have moved right over his head. A thunderstorm had already started. A few leaves from the sirish tree blew in from the window facing the verandah.

Ramdhan desperately hunted for the flute. Below the bed, under the pillow, inside the table drawer, at the bay window.

Suddenly, he heard footsteps on the stairs. He was sure it was Khageshbabu, returning to avoid being caught in the rain. He turned cold as he recalled the ten-year-old incident. The footsteps had now reached the door. Ramdhan thought about escaping from the verandah window, but he felt paralysed. And he still hadn't found his flute.

The lock clicked and the door opened. Ramdhan stood like a wooden statue, ready to face any consequences.

But somehow his predictions didn't come true. On the contrary, when Khageshbabu saw Ramdhan, his eyes turned to the ceiling and he collapsed on the floor. At that precise moment, Ramdhan's flute fell out from his coat pocket and rolled away from him. Ramdhan picked it up, jumped over Khageshbabu's body, dashed out of the door and ran down the stairs.

Ramdhan was so used to being rebuked, he never realized that Khageshbabu would, of course, have reacted this way. Ten years ago, on a stormy evening like this one, a balloon-sized hail had struck Ramdhan, spliced his head open and killed him on the spot. Khageshbabu's imposing personality notwithstanding, it was not surprising that he fell down in a swoon upon meeting the spirit of Ramdhan.

9

Master Angshuman[*]

I

I can never forget that morning. It was a Sunday. After three consecutive cloudy days, it had turned out bright and sunny. Bishuda arrived just as I had shut my notebook after completing my arithmetic homework. Bishuda, Bishwanath Ganguly, is my paternal cousin, much older than me. He works with a film company. No sooner had he come than Bishuda asked, 'Hey! When does your puja holidays begin?'

I said, 'From 7 October. Why?'

'Because I plan to whisk you away.'

'What do you mean?'

'Wait, let me first speak with your father.'

---

[*] First published in the annual *Desh*, 1985

My father was reading a newspaper in the next room. Bishuda walked up to him and I followed. Raising his head from the paper, my father said, 'Hello, Bishu, what brings you here so early in the day?'

When I heard Bishuda's reply, my heart began to beat rapidly. 'I've come to discuss an important matter with you, Chhotka,' said Bishuda. 'Our director, Sushil Mitra, is making a film. A majority of the shooting will take place in Ajmer. There is the role of a twelve-year-old boy—a substantial part, about twenty days of work. I believe Angshu will fit the role very well. If only you . . .'

'Why just me,' said my father, 'doesn't my son also hold an opinion?'

I knew my father said this in jest yet I could also feel that he had no strong objections to the idea. I know my father was very fond of acting. It was he who had taught me to recite in a free, open and uninhibited voice. Whenever I win prizes in recitation in school it's my father who is the most pleased.

'Will he have to skip school?' asked my father.

'Maybe, but not for more than two to four days,' said Bishuda. 'One-third of the work will be done during the puja vacation; after which there might be a schedule of four to five days' shooting in the Calcutta studio. Angshu is an intelligent boy—a few days of absence from school won't harm him in any way.'

'You're so keen on Angshu, will he be able to handle it?'

‘Definitely,’ said Bishuda. ‘But my own recommendation is not enough. Tomorrow morning I’m going to bring Sushil Mitra here . . . our director. But I know his nature very well. I’m sure he’ll approve of Angshu. The role is also very interesting. All actions revolve around this boy. He’ll get his script well in advance; you can coach him as well. He’ll face no problem. That apart, along with work, he can also visit new places, isn’t that an added bonus? Hey Angshu, would you have any objections in coming along with me? But your parents won’t be with you.’

I nodded my head to say I had no problem. I simply couldn’t find my voice. My heart was beating very fast.

Thanks to Bishuda I’ve already had the experience of watching a film shoot in progress. I know the drill in general. While watching a shoot a thought had often crossed my mind—I too could take part in this. I would not be scared of facing the camera. There would be no need for retakes on my account. Of course, I really don’t know how far my confidence was justified.

Bishuda said once again, ‘You need not worry. You’ll face no difficulty in doing this. And after it is completed and the film is released, you will become famous. Perhaps Master Angshuman Ganguly might even walk away with the best child actor award!’

The next day the director, Sushilbabu, came to check me out. Even though he looked very serious, he didn’t seem very strict. Upon his request I recited a Tagore’ poem,

'The Old Retainer'. The gentleman seemed quite pleased with my performance.

'I will arrange for your screen test within a few days,' said Sushilbabu. 'Bishu will keep you informed about this. I'll send across a few lines to you. Please memorize them.'

After Sushilbabu left, my father said, 'Look, son, this too is some kind of a test for you. Just as you fare well in your school exams, you need to perform well here as well. Just as your school has teachers, here the director becomes your teacher. Do listen to him. As you memorize your lessons for school, likewise here too you will need to remember all the lines of your role.'

I was afraid that my mother may put a spanner in the works but she too readily agreed. Initially she was a bit uneasy as her boy would be away for almost a month but both my parents were so fond of Bishuda and trusted him so implicitly that they both felt it was safe to leave me in his care.

That I had already acquired the part and the camera test was only a formality was confirmed when Bishuda came over with a tailor two days later to take my measurements. I would need to wear a Rajasthani dress—a kurta with narrow pyjamas. This was not the only dress I would need. I had to perform two roles: one would be that of Amrit Singh, the son of Raja Bharat Singh, and the other would be of Mohan, the son of a poor schoolmaster, Gopinath. They were both of the same age, and looked the same. They get to meet each other at the Pushkar fair. One needs to resort to camera tricks to project two identical faces together on the screen at the same time. The two new friends leave this fair and go to a quiet area to play together. There they exchange their clothes just for fun. As a result, mistaking Mohan as the prince, three gangsters kidnap him. Their sole aim is to extract a hefty sum of money from the king in exchange for the boy. Meanwhile, Amrit returns home in Mohan's clothes and discloses everything to his parents. The parents heave a sigh of relief to find that their boy has had a narrow escape but Amrit stands his ground and declares firmly that till his friend is rescued he will not talk to anyone. Finally, at the end the hero of the story, a young police inspector named Suryakant Rathore—riding a bike and displaying utmost courage—rescues the boy from the clutches of the hooligans.

Once I had heard the story and read the script of my dual role my excitement increased by leaps and bound and with it so many questions rose in my mind. In particular, I was curious to find out about the actor who would play the role of this extremely courageous Suryakant. Bishuda said that a new actor, Shankar Mallik, was being considered for that part. He was both smart and good looking. I said, 'But does he know how to ride a bike?'

With a smile Bishuda said, 'Yes, he does, but for those tricks we'll be hiring a professional stuntman from Bombay.'

'Stuntman? Now what's that?'

'You will get to see this in due course,' said Bishuda.

On 5 October our team left for Ajmer. We would board the train from Howrah to Delhi, then Delhi to Bandikui, and finally from Bandikui to Ajmer. This required changing of trains twice during the journey. Leaving on the fifth, we would reach on the night of the seventh. The bogey had already been booked in advance. Apart from the helpers everyone managed to fit into a first-class compartment. I finally met up with everyone in the train. Among the actors seven of us were at present travelling as our work would be needed right in the beginning. The rest would arrive later. The roles of Amrit Singh's mother and father, that is, the king and the queen would be played by Pulakesh Banerjee and Mamata Sen. I've already mentioned that Shankar Mallik had been cast for the role of the inspector. There was also Jagannath Dey who would be performing the part of the hooligan, Chhaganlal. Jagannath Dey is famous as the bad guy, aka the villain, in the Bengali film industry. Everyone refers to him as Jogu Ustad. Other than the actors, those who were travelling included the director, Sushilbabu; the sound recordist, Ujjwal Pramanik; the cameraman, Dhiren Bose; the writer of the story, Sukanta Gupta; and the makeup man, Sajal Sakar. The group of assistants added up to eight and finally there was Bishuda. Soon after the train left, the fourteen members of the group divided themselves into two rooms and began to play cards. Seven of them were playing rummy and the other seven, flash. As I was familiar with rummy I spent most of the time in that room. Bishuda too had joined the rummy gang. Sushilbabu and Sukanta Gupta were not playing. They were discussing the film. Pulakesh Banerjee and Mamata Sen were leafing through magazines.

Bishuda has already handed me my part in Calcutta. There are at least twenty foolscap sheets inside a file. My father had read it out to me once. I had a fair idea about how I needed to act out my role. As there are not too many words, I would face no difficulty in memorizing the lines. My screen test had been organized in a Calcutta studio two days before we left. I had to face the camera, dressed in my Rajasthani costume, and act with Shankar Mallik in a small scene. I must have delivered well, otherwise why would Sushilbabu pat me on my back and remark, 'Excellent!' Ever since, I've noticed that each time Sushilbabu caught my eye he smiled at me.

After having a 'thali' dinner at Bardhwan station I perched on the upper berth, stretched out my bedding and lay down. Mamata Sen was also travelling in my compartment. She said, 'From now on please call me Mamata Aunty, right? And if you need anything please let me know.'

As I lay down, I began to think. So much could happen in the next month. As Bishuda was accompanying me I would hardly feel the absence of my parents. I'd once gone to Kalimpong with my cousins. My parents had not been with me on that trip. I had faced no difficulty. I know this time too I would have no problem. A month would simply fly by in work.

Thinking thus I drifted off to sleep.

II

My father teaches history in a college. He had told me that Akbar had annexed Ajmer from the Marwar ruler Maldeo in the sixteenth century. In the beginning of the nineteenth century, Ajmer came under the rule of the British. Pushkar was 11 kilometres to the west of Ajmer. It is a major centre of pilgrimage for the Hindus. There's a lake here around which a fair takes place in October and is attended by lakhs of people. But in our film this city becomes the imaginary city of Hindolgarh. The name of our film is also *Hindolgarh*. Pushkar remains Pushkar and it's at the Pushkar fair that the schoolmaster's son, Mohan, meets the prince, Amrit Singh.

After reaching Ajmer late at night we headed for the circuit house. It would be our base for the next three weeks. It was a pretty large circuit house. On the north and west side of the first floor was a broad verandah from where you could see the huge Ana Sagar Lake to the north and the mountain range to the west. At night of course there was nothing to see but there was no escaping the feeling that we were in a strange house at a very strange place.

The reflection of the moon on the lake visible through the thin veneer of the fog looked magical. The faraway sound of a song and drums seemed to be coming from another city. There was no other sound.

I was standing next to the verandah railing when Bishuda walked up and said, 'Come! Your room is ready. Mamatadi too will sleep in the same room. You have no reason to fear.'

In any case I wasn't afraid of anything. I would be staying together with so many people, what was there to fear?

'When will my work begin?' I asked Bishuda.

He said, 'Tomorrow we'll visit Pushkar and check out the house which will serve as our palace. The work begins from the day after.'

As we were talking, Mamata Aunty burst into our conversation and said, 'Hello, Angshu! Missing your mother?'

To be frank not once had I thought of home and that was exactly what I told her.

'That's the spirit,' said Mamata Aunty. 'While we are here, consider me your mother, right? If you face any problem please come to me.'

I slept soundly that night.

In the morning when I again went out to the verandah I finally saw the lake. It was so huge that the buildings on the other side looked tiny. Numerous ducks floated about.

The mountain seemed huge. It seemed to emerge straight out of the water.

After a sumptuous breakfast of bread, eggs and large-sized jalebis, at 9 we went to see the diamond merchant Swaruplal Lohia's house. The majority of the people in our team stayed back at the circuit house. Only six of us were going on this trip—myself, Bishuda, Sushilbabu, Sushilbabu's assistant Mukul Chaudhury, cameraman Dheeresh Bose and the writer of the film, Sukanta Gupta. A bus and three taxis have been rented for three weeks, of which only two taxis were on duty today.

It would be wrong to call Lohia's residence a house. It was more like a fortress. There was no moat round the building but the entire complex was massive, including trees, a pond, a temple and a huge expanse of land. This fortress would turn into our palace and Amrit Singh would be the son of its king and queen.

To be honest I had never seen a house like this. It was made of yellow stone. You couldn't predict how old it was. It could jolly well belong to the Mughal period. Eventually this turned out to be true.

Mr Lohia was above sixty. He had dazzling white hair and a twirling moustache. He received us cordially and took us to his drawing room. He said he did not watch too many films. But he was very fond of Bengal and of Bengalis. One of his maternal cousins has been settled in business in Calcutta over the last 200 years. Our producer was familiar with this brother, Motilal Chunauria. It was he who had written a letter to Mr Lohia and helped arrange for our shooting. One advantage of this house was that the rooms outnumbered the people who lived in it. If we used some of the rooms to shoot, it would not disturb the other people of the house.

Mr Lohia treated us to tea and laddoos and then showed us his jewel collection. My eyes widened at the display. Towards the end he showed us a blue stone which was almost the size of a pigeon egg. It was named lapis lazuli. Stones of this size were rarely found. I was very keen to inquire about the price and Sushilbabu finally posed this query. Mr Lohia smiled and replied, 'It is priceless.' No wonder he had employed armed security guards outside his house. It contained jewels amounting to crores.

After bidding farewell to Mr Lohia we headed for Pushkar. On the way we crossed a gorge which was a mile long. There were high mountains on both sides and the lake appeared in between the rocks. It took us twenty minutes to reach Pushkar.

Sukantababu is an avid reader. He had already read up a lot on Rajasthan. He said that Pushkar had been a major centre of pilgrimage in India over a century ago too. Aurangzeb had destroyed the temples beside the lake and in its place new temples had been built. Among them the most famous was the temple dedicated to Brahma. In fact this was the only temple in India where Brahma was

worshipped. Outside the temple the figure of a swan could be seen, symbolizing Brahma's carrier. Sushilbabu and Sukantababu went inside the temple to pay their respects.

The Pushkar fair was due to start in two days' time. Arrangements had been made on a massive open space on the southern side of the lake. Camels, cows and horses had begun arriving. There was no other market where these three animals were brought and sold together. Sushilbabu and the cameraman, Dheeresh Bose, chose an area on the opposite side of the fair with a few trees around an old ruined haveli to shoot the scenes of Amrit and Mohan exchanging clothes as well as the kidnapping sequence. It was from this spot that those three ruffians would pick up Mohan, wearing Amrit's clothes, and flee. Of course these villains did not belong to earlier times. They, along with Mohan, would escape in a car and not on a camel or horseback.

By the time we returned from Pushkar it was past noon. Lunch had been organized on the first floor dining hall of the circuit house. About fifteen people, including the hero and villains, were having lunch. The atmosphere reminded you of a picnic full of jollity. This routine would continue while we stayed in Ajmer. Once our work started our stay at the circuit house would be limited to a few hours as we would be spending most of our time outside.

While having his lunch Sushilbabu began talking about Mr Lohia's jewel collection. The others who had stayed behind were full of regret at not having seen this amazing thing, the lapis lazuli.

After lunch I went through the script for the next day's shooting. I was aware that shooting never followed the sequence of the plot. Very often the scenes which were to appear at the end are shot first and vice versa. Like the scene which would be first shot tomorrow would include the scene of our return from the fair. Though it was the first day's work, it would not be that easy. When I opened the file to familiarize myself with tomorrow's part, Bishuda turned up to say that a rehearsal would be held in the verandah in the evening. The king, the queen, the raja's manager and I were required to attend. I said to myself that here began my work.

Who knew that so much adventure was to follow? Who knew that much action, drama and mindboggling mystery, not part of the shooting script, were to dog us all through our stay here.

III

The next day I had to get up at 6 a.m. Not just I, Panchanan, the bearer, woke up the others who were required for the day's shooting and offered them tea. Breakfast was to follow. This was perhaps bed-tea. Though not quite habituated to this yet I quite liked drinking this morning tea. Given the nip in the air in Ajmer in October, Mamata Aunty forced a pullover on me. I could always take it off when the sun grew stronger.

We had a good rehearsal yesterday. Whatever apprehension I had had vanished as I began working with the others. Three local Bengalis have been recruited for a few small roles required in the palace. They all are old-time residents of Ajmer. Bishuda himself located them. As production manager, Bishuda has to be on his feet all day. This one individual never has time to rest.

Today work was to start at 9 in the morning. There would be a break for an hour at 1'o clock and then work would resume once more at 2 p.m. My work would be over by evening. Shooting would continue after sundown too, involving the three hooligans, and I would be required for just one shot. This was roughly the sequence to be shot: Chhaganlal, the rogue, and his two aides hang around outside the palace, waiting for an opportunity to capture the prince Amrit Singh and flee. They spot Amrit Singh in a room on the second floor, moving around between different rooms. Chhaganlal catches an occasional glimpse of him.

All vehicles were required today. What was first loaded on the top of the bus were objects which looked like railway tracks for the camera to run on. There were 8-10-foot lines in separate pieces which would be joined together to make a longer track. Over this would run the wheeled motor known as a trolley, atop which would sit the camera. A trolley too was being put on the top of the bus. Large-sized studio lights were also placed on the roof. Even in daylight this extra electric light is used to shoot interior sequences to accentuate the natural light.

Apart from me the others required for the shots this morning were the king, the queen, the manager and three more people who had to say no dialogue. They were referred to as 'extras' and they all have been recruited in Ajmer itself. There's a Hindi theatre group here and they had visited the circuit house last evening. They said they could help us find people.

At 7.30, our car and the bus set off. It would take about ten minutes to reach Mr Lohia's house; thus we had plenty of time on our hands. But it also requires eons of time to organize a set. I had observed this on the day of my screen test. The person playing the role of the raja, Pulakesh Banerjee, has been in the field of acting for the last fifteen years. He is also into theatre. He was sitting next to me in the car and on our way he suggested, 'Come, Angshuman, let's go through our lines together.' I had no problem with that and we did a few rounds of rehearsal.

We had our breakfast soon after we reached the palace. Mr Lohia had given over the entire ground floor for our use. Three more rooms on the first floor have also been spared for the shoot. Each of these rooms were equipped with chairs, tables, carpets, paintings as well as a chandelier. These could all be well utilized in the film. Hardly anything had been brought along from Calcutta as home furnishings.

While we were busy with breakfast on the ground floor the shooting stuff was transferred to the rooms on the first floor. Soon after finishing their breakfast, Pulakeshbabu and Mamata Aunty left for make-up on the first floor verandah. I did not need to apply any make-up; only my hair had to be brushed in a different direction. While I was pondering over some extra time I had with me, a sound in front of the house attracted my attention. A motorcycle was roaring on to the ground with its rider—Bishuda.

After going round the grounds a couple of times, he parked the bike he parked it right in front of me and called, 'Come, sit behind me. Let me take you for a short ride.'

Since the script required me to sit on the back seat of Inspector Suryakant's motorbike, I sat on the carrier seat. Bishuda sped off with a booming noise. My hands were tightly clasped around Bishuda's waist; the wind blew sharply into my ears—how thrilling! I had no idea that Bishuda rode a bike so well. I only knew that he had been driving cars for a very long time.

After taking me for three rounds, Bishuda parked his bike in front of the house. This had been a wonderful rehearsal for me! If the stuntman was an expert, I would have no fear sitting behind him. According to the script, after rescuing Mohan from the clutches of the dacoits, Inspector Suryakant rides at breakneck speed, and the dacoits chase him in an Ambassador. In order to escape, Suryakant skips this road and lands on uneven ground. Mohan clutches on to his back as the bike gallops at tremendous speed. And then? This is the highlight . . . it will have people in cinema halls breaking out in loud applause—the car with the miscreants continues to follow him, as the *kutcha* road on which Suryakant is speeding slopes upward.

Before he starts climbing, Suryakant accelerates to the fullest. The reason is simple—right in front is a very wide ditch with water surging across. One has to jump over this canal and land on the opposite side, on the raised land. The story mentions how Suryakant does that with great ease but will the Bombay stuntman be able to enact this as effortlessly while shooting? During the real shooting do I actually have to be seated in the carrier's seat with my hands clasping the stuntman's waist?

It's best not to discuss it right now. I will get to know this nearer the time in any case. If the work demands it, for the sake of perfection I'll definitely be there in person.

After climbing down from the motorcycle Bishuda said, 'We hired this bike for Suryakant. Hopefully the captain will like it.'

'Captain?' I asked him in surprise. 'Who's this captain?'

'Captain Krishnan,' said Bishuda. 'Stuntman. He is arriving from Bombay tonight.'

Krishnan! Even though he was coming from Bombay the name suggested that he is south Indian.

IV

The first day's schedule went off smoothly. The first shot was mine—clad in Mohan's clothes I would enter a room along with the manager. My father is flummoxed to see the change of clothes. As the shot was cleared in the first take, I received an ovation from everyone present at the shoot. Mr Lohia, who had come to watch the performance with his grandson, too joined in the applause. I felt sad when I thought of my parents. Had they been present at such an enjoyable shooting it would have given them so much joy. As I had to get ready in five minutes for the second shot, however, I overcome my low mood. Bishuda was present during my first shot. After the shot he patted my back and whispered to me, 'Carry on like this. No need to worry.'

In the role of the king, Pulakesh Banerjee too performed quite well, but what he said during lunchtime amused me a lot. 'You know, Angshuman, no one notices the work of an adult artist in the presence of a child actor. Our hard work goes for a toss.' I had also noticed that Pulakeshbabu shut his eyes and mumbled to himself before each shot. Maybe he prayed to god.

I also liked Mamata Aunty's acting. Particularly the way she could bring tears to her eyes. Many actors can't cry so naturally. If a scene required the shedding of tears, they put a drop of glycerine in one corner of their eyes before the shot. The glycerine results in a burning reaction and the eyes well up with tears. Mamata Aunty said she didn't require glycerine. Much to my surprise I realized this was true indeed. When she heard that the gangsters had kidnapped the other child by mistake, and not her son, she burst into tears of sheer joy and took the boy in her arms.

The entire sequence was completed by 5 in the evening. The next shot would be set up sometime after sunset. Not before 7. Pulakeshbabu and Mamata Aunty returned to the circuit house. The rest of the work was rather easy. All I had to do was to wander about from one room to another. The camera captured this from outside the house in such a way that it would appear as if the gangsters were watching me.

Two hours were well spent in listening to the gramophone. Mr Lohia has an old gramophone with a horn and with it a huge collection of old records of both Hindi film songs as well as Hindustani classical music. He played those records for us. I had never seen a hand-cranked gramophone before. Assistant Mukul Chaudhuri is a connoisseur of classical music; he said it was no longer possible to acquire such records now. Mr Lohia has preserved them well even after many years of use.

A little before 7 p.m., I stopped listening to music and began to get ready for my next shot. This time I was in the prince's dress; it took me fifteen minutes to get ready. But then news arrived that the work would get delayed. The actor who was playing the role of Chhaganlal, Jagannath Dey or Jogu Ustad, was missing. Bishuda was checking with everyone about Jagannath. I had seen him earlier in the evening; where could the man have disappeared?

I must mention here that however great he might be as an actor, I didn't quite like Jagannath Dey as a person. Two reasons lay behind this. Firstly, I don't find his smile very pleasant. Frankly speaking, tobacco-stained teeth can never look clean. Secondly, I don't like the way he behaves with the two helpers, Bhikhu and Panchanan. I find this very unpleasant because both worked really hard.

Before he went to look for Jogu Ustad, Bishuda discussed with Sushilbabu that my bit could be shot in the meantime. I was ready; they only needed to position the lights. As it's not possible to work just with available normal lights, high-voltage lights are used in studios. Sushilbabu explained how I should move between the rooms. 'You can hum a song to yourself and match your step to the beat. Then your walk will appear normal and relaxed. As the prince has nothing much to do at this point, he just wanders aimlessly around the different rooms. This mood should reflect in your action.'

I can sing a bit but couldn't decide which number to hum. When I asked Sushilbabu he thought for a moment and said, 'Can you sing "*Aaj Dhaaner Khete Raudra Chhayaye*"?'

When I said yes, Sushilbabu said, 'Very good. Then you hum along that song.'

I now sang the song to myself. I didn't remember all the words but there was no need for them either.

We were done with the shot in half an hour. Another half an hour later, Bishuda arrived to say that Jogu Ustad had been found. Bishuda was hopping mad, and so I did not ask him much. I gathered from snatches of conversation that Jogu was much too fond of drink. He had gone to a local liquor shop in the market situated a little away from the palace. After sundown it appeared that he could not do without a drink.

Meanwhile, the other two miscreants were already ready for the shot; now Jogu Ustad had to put on make-up and his costume to turn into Chhaganlal. This took almost another hour. In between Bishuda came to check if I wanted to return to my room. As I found everything so interesting, I said I wouldn't return without seeing this dacoit sequence being shot.

By the time the shot was taken it was 9.30 p.m. The three ruffians were waiting under a tree right next to the palace wall. As the wall was very high only the summit of the palace could be seen. Chhaganlal climbed up the tree deftly.

The other two followed. They could now see Amrit clearly. At this critical moment a security guard came into sight. Hearing him shout, the three of them jumped from the tree and ran to the car to escape.

After watching the sequence I realized that irrespective of Jogu Ustad being an alcoholic or not he definitely was an expert actor. Later Bishuda had told me, 'This fellow is a tremendous actor. That's why one can't help but turn to him despite his wayward ways.' I told myself, do whatever, but when you come to act with me please don't come drunk. I've heard that alcohol produces a terrible stench.

V

Having reached the circuit house quite late at night I felt a bit tired. I went to sleep right after dinner. I did not need to wake up too early the next day as only the crowd at the Pushkar fair would be shot in the morning and none of the actors were required. As the fair would start from tomorrow it was best to capture a few shots now before it got too crowded. There was work in the evening at the palace. The presence of the hero, Shankar Mallik, would be required this time. The scene would be—after the king informs the police, Inspector Suryakant comes to question Amrit and gathers all information. Therefore, Pulakesh Banerjee as well as myself will have work to do.

Even though there was no hurry to get up I couldn't sleep beyond 7. This worked in my favour. I met Bishuda the moment I stepped on to the verandah. Bishuda said, 'Will you come with us?'

I said, 'Where to?'

'Doural. It is 16 kilometres from here. We have found a canal as described in the story, and would like to show it to Krishnan. He needs to check if a motorcycle can jump across it or not.'

'Has the stuntman arrived?'

'Yes, indeed,' said Bishuda, The train was three hours late. I returned with Krishnan at 1.30 a.m.'

'Does it mean that a motorcycle too will travel with us?'

'Yes, definitely. It will travel on the roof of the bus. He'll use it when we reach the location.'

'Which region does Krishnan belong to? Is he from Madras?'

'You can figure this out only when you meet him.'

I finished my breakfast by 8. Today we have only the bus with us as the other three cars have left for Pushkar for the shoot. Everyone seemed to be interested in this outing. All those who hadn't gone for the shooting hopped into the bus. At the end one fellow arrived with Bishuda. He was about thirty years old, with a clear complexion and slightly above-average height. The gentleman appeared very fit and able. This was clear from the way he carried himself.

'You were so keen to find out about the stuntman—here he is. Captain Krishnan,' called Bishuda, inviting him to sit on the empty seat next to me. Captain Krishnan turned towards me and, flashing his bright teeth, said in clear Bengali, 'Namaskar.'

This took me by real surprise. I had no idea that a Bengali could have a name like Krishnan.

The motorcycle had been loaded atop the bus. After blowing the horn twice the deluxe bus set off.

Everyone in the bus was turning around to look at the stuntman. My eyes too were fixed on him. The gentleman was now quietly smiling to himself. After a while I couldn't help but ask him, 'You seem to be a Bengali, but your name is—?'

'My name is Krishnapada Sanyal,' the gentleman said with a smile. 'In Bombay no one gives any importance to a Bengali stuntman. Hence, I've adopted a south Indian name. There I speak in broken Hindi and English. I don't need to speak very often—no one pays any heed to our words; they only want to check out our action.'

I found everything so strange about this gentleman. As Shankar Mallik, he will be the one performing the complicated stunts while the audience will happily assume it has all been done by Shankar Mallik. Bishuda had once told me, 'All these Hindi film heroes fighting, falling off horses, dashing across rooftops—it's all done by the stuntmen yet the public don't really know the real picture.'

I glanced at the gentleman once more. Krishnapada Sanyal. He seemed to belong to a well-to-do family. How could a member of such a family become a stuntman? I must find out these details from him. I could see that if he sported a moustache, no one would be able to make out any difference between him and Shankar Mallik from a distance. They shared the same physique and complexion. Must compliment Bishuda on his choice. I know that it's he who had arranged for him as the stuntman.

'What's your name?'

I answered. Then I said, 'I think I may have to sit behind you on the bike.'

'Yes, you will,' said Captain Krishnan. 'There's no need to fear. No one can perform such motorcycle stunts like me.

I've ridden motorcycles in twenty-two Hindi and Tamil films, and not once have I failed.'

'Is that so?'

'Yes, sir.'

I took a liking to him. You don't usually see such a confident man. Anyone whose smile was so genuine could never be so crooked. I don't think so.

As I heard Captain Krishnan beginning to hum a Hindi song, I didn't disturb him further. I would have plenty of time to get to know him. The sequence involving the jump over the canal would be shot two weeks later.

Doural is a small town. The bus left the city and after a while Bishuda instructed it to stop at a certain place. On the left there was a walking track that ran through the forest. It was clear that a bus could not travel through this. Yet we had to use this track. Sushilbabu, Bishuda and the cameraman had already made a trip to Ajmer last month for a recce. Locations had to be scouted well beforehand. Once the shooting began there was little time for such activities. The director had approved the canal but the person who had to perform the stunt on a bike needed to inspect it too!

Bishuda said, 'You need to walk for five minutes from the main road to reach the spot. A jeep could probably go through but certainly not a car or bus.'

Climbing down from the bus, we began to walk. The motorcycle was brought down. Captain Krishnan mounted it and switched the ignition on. The bike came to life with a loud noise and he began to ride alongside us.

It was a sparse forest and we weren't familiar with the trees at all. But it bore little resemblance to the Bengal landscape. In due course the sounds from the main road died down completely. Now it was only the thud of the bike and the chirping of birds.

After a few minutes we heard a stream gushing. It was clear that we had reached the canal. Here the path was a little broad and somewhat uphill. It rose for a bit and then descended suddenly to merge with the canal. Even though the canal was ten metres wide, the motorcycle required a run of at least twenty metres at this end to accelerate and reach the other end of the canal.

'So what do you think of this, Captain?' Bishuda walked up to Krishnan and asked him.

Krishnan got off his bike and walked around to inspect the canal from up close.

'Let me check on the other side once.'

Krishnan went down the slope, reached the edge of the canal, rolled up his trousers and waded across the water to reach the other side. After observing the other side for a few minutes he returned and said, 'I'll give it a try once. All of you please stand to one side.'

Everyone in the group went down the slope, jostling, and positioned themselves across the two sides of the path to the canal. I was with the group on the left side and kept

my gaze intent on the road. Krishnan meanwhile walked up and reached his bike. As there was a bush on the other side of the road, we were unable to see Krishnan but we could hear the bike roaring. As the sound faded, I could sense that Krishnan was taking his bike farther away to help him accelerate.

'Please indicate when you're ready,' shouted Bishuda.

The reply arrived within a few seconds. 'Ready. I'm coming.'

Now that the sound of the bike began to grow louder, I realized that Krishnan was on the move. It took him three seconds to appear from behind the bush from the time he took off—and then came the spellbinding action. Like a hungry tiger exerting all his strength to jump on to his prey from a distance of ten metres, Captain Krishnan's motorbike leapt into the air with the same grace and alacrity, crossed over the canal and landed on the opposite uphill path before disappearing behind a bush.

Each member of the team broke out in spontaneous applause to hail Krishnan's amazing stunt.

But it did not end there. I'll never forget what followed. I suddenly heard Krishnan's voice from the other side.

'Master Angshuman!'

I don't know why but hearing my name left me baffled. As if the name belonged to someone else.

'Where are you, Master Angshuman?' he called once more.

Meanwhile, Bishuda was coming towards me.

'He is calling for you. Will you go?'

'I'll go.'

All my fears vanished like magic. Something told me that there was nothing to be afraid of with Captain Krishnan as the charioteer.

I shouted back, 'I'm coming right away.' Thereafter, I rolled up my trousers, crossed over the canal and arrived on the other side. About twenty metres away, Captain Krishnan was sitting on his bike. He beckoned to me with a wave.

'Let's have a rehearsal!'

I went towards Captain Krishnan. He patted the pillion and indicated where I had to sit. I sat down.

'There's no need to be frightened. Clasp my waist tightly with your hands.'

I held on to him. Captain Krishnan turned his bike around and took it farther from the canal. Then he started easing the bike forward, before accelerating and taking off, the engine roaring.

I clasped his waist and shut my eyes. Hence, I didn't see anything, but when I opened my eyes, I realized that we were on the other side. It seemed like I had been in the middle of a tornado! Everyone clapped once more and cheered him.

'How was that?' asked Captain Krishnan.

I said, 'That was great fun; very relaxing.'

'Good, there's no need to worry now. Bishubabu had described the scene to me on our way from the station. I had said, "There's no reason to be anxious. If the boy has no problem sitting on my bike, I have nothing to worry about."'

In the meantime, a whole lot of people had gathered around us. Sushilbabu was busy shooting in Pushkar, otherwise he too would have been very happy and relieved. Shankar Mallik patted me on my back and praised me by saying 'brave boy'. He then introduced himself to Captain Krishnan, shook hands with him and said, 'I was a bit nervous about this stunt. I'm aware that I need to do nothing yet I was worried whether the person doing it would resemble me or not. But seeing you, I realize you just need to add a moustache and no one will be able to make out any difference between us.'

Mission completed, everyone boarded the bus. By noon we needed to be back for our lunch at the circuit house and then we would leave for Mr Lohia's house.

I felt very relieved that the rehearsal of the stunt had gone so smoothly. This would be my most difficult scene in the entire film and I had been worked up over it. Thank god we had found Krishnan. I realized the value of a good stuntman.

VI

The work in Mr Lohia's house scheduled in the afternoon was completed by 5 p.m. I was particularly happy now as there had been no retakes for any mistake. Now I know that if you can get over the fear of the camera, your work becomes much easier. The hero, Shankar Mallik, performed very well on the first day. No one knew much about him as he too was a newcomer. Later, Shankarbabu himself told us that he was addicted to movies. He had watched several foreign films. This must have helped him immensely because what he delivered today hardly looked like acting. A real-life police inspector, Mr Maheshwari, a close friend of Mr Lohia's, had come to watch us shoot.

He was very happy to see the shooting and praised everyone before he left.

In the evening, after I returned to the circuit house, I met Captain Krishnan once again. I had thought of him and of his impressive act all afternoon. I know very well that if my parents were here, they would have never allowed me to do such a thing. Bishuda told me, 'When you write home, please don't mention this stunt. Aunty and Uncle should know about this only when they watch the film. Not before. If they find out, I won't hear the end of it.

'How was the shoot?' Captain Krishnan asked me.

'It was good. But nothing to match this morning's canal episode.'

'One thing,' said Krishnan, 'from now on please call me Keshtoda. That's my real name. There's no reason why I should keep up my south Indian persona with you.'

This suited me just fine. I too was keen to call Captain Krishnan 'dada' but had not known how to initiate it.

I also wished to ask him something and I decided to do so now.

'How did you become a stuntman, Keshtoda?'

'It's a long story,' said Keshtoda. 'I come from an academic family in Konnogor. My father was a Sanskrit and mathematics teacher in a school. He must be still around. I was a kid who often bunked school. I would skip classes and go to watch Hindi action films and would then get beaten up by my father. Often with a stick. But I'd picked up a trick or two so that it never hurt me much even if he hit me on my back. My father wasn't that strong anyway. My grandfather was. He too was a Sanskrit scholar but he exercised regularly. He swung clubs. Once, a ram charged at him. He charged back at the ram and snapped its horns. That should give you an idea about how strong he was. I was also into exercise but if you work too much on your muscles it interferes with the art of stunts. The body should be like a spring. When you fall down, your body should relax. That way, the damage to your bones will be far less. Over the past ten years I've fallen off a horse's back at least five hundred times. It's not that I never got hurt. My body is full of scratch marks. But during a shot no one else ever realizes if I am injured or not.'

Keshtoda stopped for a few moments. Then he lit a cigarette and began to speak again.

'I left school at the age of thirteen. My father gave up on me. I ran away from home. Reaching Calcutta, I took up a job as a waiter in Tower Hotel in Sealdah. After working for five years I saved 156 rupees and on a sudden impulse bought a third-class ticket and boarded the Bombay Mail. It took me two days to reach Bombay. It was a bustling city and I didn't know a soul and had only heard of Bombay Talkies. It was only after reaching there did I realize that Bombay Talkies did not exist any more. Now where do I head? After wandering about and talking to a few people I finally arrived at Rajkamal Studio in Parel. I came to know that a Bengali director, Swadesh Mukherjee, was shooting there. Without giving the matter much thought I entered the studio and stood quietly in one corner.

'That this fellow was a real gentleman will be apparent from the story I'll tell you now. A fight between a hero and villain was being shot. The stuntmen had taken their place. The hero's stuntman had to fling himself on the floor after being kicked on his stomach. I'd practised falling down in a similar manner on the terrace of the hotel in Calcutta. I was hiding myself in the crowd just to see how such a scene was enacted here. But what ensued was a disaster. As a result of a slight miscalculation, the hero's stuntman hit his head against the corner of a table as he fell. The outcome was an instant blackout. He had to be lifted up and carried out of the studio. Meanwhile, both the director and the producer started to panic. Work would come to a halt in the absence of a stuntman. Not being able to shoot even for a day costs the producer Rs 20,000. Without giving a thought to the possible consequences, I approached the director. In a mix of broken Hindi and English I told him that my name was Unni Krishnan, that I belonged to Malabar and was a stuntman. I requested them to try me out.

'The situation was so precarious that no one berated me for entering a studio without permission. The director right away suggested a rehearsal with me and said that if I cleared it, I would be taken on.

'Gritting my teeth I took the plunge. Rehearsal perfect, take perfect. Captain Krishnan was born that day. But what I learnt the hard way was that no one becomes famous in this field. No one knows the name of a stuntman in a fight sequence. Yet if one survives there's no dearth of work. The demand for stunts is constantly going up. In one film I had to hang from a rope tied to a helicopter. One stunt—Rs 20,000. You're playing with your life after all. Each stunt is life threatening. Your life is at stake with each stunt—one slip and you are either dead or grievously injured. You yourself saw this morning how risky the whole affair was. Suppose I'd messed up, you can imagine what would have happened.'

I could imagine, but I didn't want to. I knew that my luck was now intertwined with Keshtoda's. I'd no choice to retract from this nor did I wish to.

In the twilight the last swathes of colours vanished from behind the mountain range. The lake turned dark blue. One could still see the ducks but they would not be visible for much longer. Everyone had settled down to play cards inside. This was obvious from the raucous laughter one could hear.

I asked, 'Don't you play cards, Keshtoda?'

'I do,' said Keshtoda. 'I was playing this afternoon with . . . oh well . . . a fellow from your group whom you call Jogu Ustad—who is he?'

'He is playing the main villain. He is quite a well-known actor. His real name is Jagannath Dey.'

'It's been years since I have watched any Bengali film.'

'But why do you mention him?

'Because he too was present at the card game. He called me in when I was sitting in my room. He is not the most honest of guys. A big-time cheat. But it's not so easy to fool me. I could see through his act in the second round. But I found his reaction rather unpleasant. I've rarely heard any person resort to such verbal abuse. He is not a decent guy.'

I knew this too well and narrated yesterday's incident to Keshtoda.

'Hmm . . .' said Keshtoda, preoccupied. Then he said, 'Don't you have your parents in Calcutta?'

I said, 'Yes. And I also have an older sister who's now married. '

'Don't you miss you parents?'

'Nope. Now that you're here I will miss them even less.'

'Good. We must ensure that we accomplish our work well. Please pay attention to your work. And if you do, you'll build a good name for yourself. With you, it's clearly possible.'

'Why just me, you will too.'

Keshtoda shook his head.

'No way. Stuntmen must forgo credit. If anyone earns a name it is the hero, and that gives us the satisfaction.'

Keshtoda got up.

'Let me see if I can gatecrash any of the card parties.'

VII

After three days my most enjoyable experience of shooting took place at the Pushkar fair. This was the first instance where I had to perform in a dual role. The scene of a conversation between Mohan and Amrit was shot twice. At first, I acted as Mohan and in front of me stood Shyamsundar, a local boy aged twelve, who took Amrit's place. The second time, I acted as Amrit and the same boy stood in place of Mohan. When people watch these scenes on the screen they won't get to see Shyamsundar at all. Instead they'll see Mohan and Amrit talking to each other.

There was not much crowd at the fair when we shot the kidnapping sequence. Otherwise, it would have been a huge problem. Jogu Ustad doesn't drink in the morning. Therefore, he performed the part of Chhaganlal rather well. But he could have tackled the scene where he picks up Amrit attired in Mohan's clothes and flings him inside the car more carefully. It hurt my hip and the pain continued till evening.

When I returned to the circuit house in the evening, I met Keshtoda. Over the past two days all shooting had taken place inside the palace from dawn to dusk. Keshtoda was also present but I had not come across him after work. Having reached the circuit house late at night I had been exhausted, taken a bath, had dinner and gone right off to sleep. I was curious to find out if any incident worth reporting had taken place over the past two days. I received my answer that evening.

Though Keshtoda was humming a tune to himself I could make out from the scowl on his face that something was bothering him.

'I was looking for you,' Keshtoda said.

'Why, what's the matter,' I asked.

'It's serious.'

'Tell me.'

'You were shooting in the palace for the past two days. As I didn't have much to do, I was hanging about here and there. I also visited a few sites of Ajmer. Yesterday at 8 in the evening I went to the market. I thought it would be nice to have a cup of hot tea. I'd already noticed this teashop before. As I was seated outside on a bench sipping my tea, I saw two men come out of the next shop. It was a liquor shop. One of the two was your Jogu Ustad and the other was someone I had seen at the palace where he works as a servant. His name is probably Vikram. The moment I spotted the servant with Jogu Ustad something made me uneasy. They did not however leave the place immediately. Talking to each other, they disappeared into the darkness behind the shop.

'Curious, I too got up from the bench and followed them cautiously. A bullock cart was parked between

the two shops. I went near it and concealed myself well. I heard Jogu Ustad's voice. I realized he was asking Vikram to help him with some work. If Vikram did the job well he promised a handsome amount. They had an argument over the amount and finally settled at Rs 1000. It clearly implied that they were planning to steal something from the fortress. This servant would steal the stuff, hand it over to Jogu Ustad and would receive the amount of Rs 1000.'

It was clear to me. The lapis lazuli. It had often been discussed in the presence of Jogu Ustad. He was perfectly aware of its real value. He was planning to steal it with the help of the servant. And now Keshtoda knew about the plan as well.

After I told Keshtoda all about the lapis lazuli, I asked him, 'Hope they didn't realize that you've heard them.'

'I don't think so,' said Keshtoda. 'I didn't stay too long. I slipped away the moment I gauged the situation. Now the problem is how does one handle this?'

'Do you think we should tell Bishuda?'

Keshtoda shook his head. 'That won't help. Jogu Ustad is yet to finish his work. If he hadn't started shooting, he could have been replaced. Now there'll be this issue of continuity.'

'What's that?'

'Continuity. Since he has worked for three days, he has now established himself as Chhaganlal. If one uses another actor, we will need to reshoot those three days with the new fellow. This will lead to losses running into lakhs. Jogu knows this and is taking advantage. He knows he is indispensable. He is encashing on this opportunity.'

'What then?'

'Just keep your lips sealed and let's just hope that they are unable to steal it. The stone you're referring to . . . how big is it?'

'Almost the size of a pigeon's egg.'

'What is its value?'

'It is beyond estimation. Or in other words it's invaluable.'

'Oh dear!'

Keshtoda left with a grim face.

Before going to bed I stepped out in the verandah after dinner. It was a sparkling moonlit night. The water of the lake was shimmering. Just then I heard a sound and turned around.

Someone else was in the verandah.

Jogu Ustad. I was taken aback. He was walking towards me. What did he want from me? By now he must be drunk. The verandah will start reeking.

No, there was no smell. He looked sober.

'How are you, my boy?'

What an odd question!

I said, 'Why, I'm fine.'

'After the afternoon shot, I saw you rub your back. Hope you're not terribly hurt?'

'No, no. There is no more pain.'

'Very good. I was a bit worried about you. So I thought I'd check on you.'

'I'm quite fine.'

Jogu Ustad left.

Today this gentleman seemed so different.

Had Keshtoda heard right?

VIII

Seven days passed by.

The shooting was progressing well. As everyone was now familiar with the logistics, work was moving ahead speedily. In the meantime I've received letters from my parents. They were happy to hear that my work was going well.

Apart from Bishuda there were a few others who asked about my well-being every other day. One of them of course was Mamata Aunty. She clearly understood how a mother's absence mattered. To be honest, it was good to have her around otherwise it would have become very difficult to pay attention to everything. Then there was Sushilbabu who, though generally a bit reserved, would often come up once at least and ask, 'Is everything all right?' Among his assistants, I was particularly fond of Mukul Chaudhuri. He always looked out for me when I was giving a shot. Suppose in one shot the top button of my kurta was open, it was his responsibility to ensure that this was maintained in other shots of the same scene.

I was further convinced that Keshtoda was wrong when seven days in a row I spotted nothing suspicious in Jogu Ustad's attitude. I haven't had the chance yet but when I meet Keshtoda next I decided to tell him this.

Over the next seven days the work on the film proceeded very well. Both Pulakesh Banerjee and Mamata

Aunty had finished their work that morning and would return to Calcutta in the evening. Meanwhile, an Ajmer-based forty-year-old Bengali actor had been located to play Mohan's poor schoolmaster father. He had already shot for one day. Keshtoda shot for three more days out of which one day he worked on a fight sequence with another newly arrived stuntman. On screen it would be a fight between Chhaganlal and Suryakant. One of the three villains kicks Suryakant's hand so that the pistol drops to the ground. Suryakant gets involved in fist fights to retrieve it. Jogu Ustad and Shankar Mallik had to act in the scene, using their fists, not hurting each other, with the stuntmen replacing them when they were supposed to be flung around from the blows.

For the villain's den, a 300-year-old ruined building had been selected a little away from the city. These scenes were to be shot there. I had to be part of these shots as Mohan was held hostage in the building and Inspector Suryakant had come there to rescue him. I was to be in a state of anguish as my hands and feet were all tied up and I was bundled up in one corner of a room. The work of the stuntmen took my breath away. Keshtoda's stunts in particular were matchless. There were times it almost seemed like Keshtoda had no bones in his body—otherwise, how was it possible that he felt no pain despite flinging himself on the ground time and again?

The remaining two days of Keshtoda's shoot involved me riding on his bike. Though the chase sequence with the cars and the bike would be on screen for barely a minute and a half, the number of shots required would be almost sixty to seventy. The sequence would come to an end with the scene of the bike flying across the canal. This will be shot after seven days. As this was the most demanding shot, it had been scheduled for a later date. After this shot I would be done with my work and so would Keshtoda.

One had to admit that when it came to acting, Jogu Ustad could scarcely be faulted. Hence, I had my doubts if Keshtoda had heard right. When he got a bit of free time on the fifth day, after an entire day's shooting on a motorcycle, Keshtoda arrived in the circuit house in the evening to meet me. I had just come to the verandah after a bath. The Ana Sagar Lake never tires you. And the sunset behind the mountain range looked gloriously different every day.

'What news?' asked Keshtoda?

I said, 'I have been waiting to hear from you.'

'I think the fellow has given up,' said Keshtoda. 'Given a chance I often drop into that teashop in the evenings. I cover up well and hide myself on the bench. I hope no one can figure me out. Disguised thus, I spotted Jogu Ustad enter the wine shop thrice. I also saw one of the other three hooligans one day but that servant, Vikram, has never visited the place again.'

'In that case you may have heard wrong.'

Keshtoda shook his head.

'No way. I did not hear wrong. They are definitely hatching a plot. One day when I did not have much to do in the palace, I went to chat up a retainer on the pretext of looking for a matchbox. He said Mr Lohia's chief bearer has been on leave for the past three weeks. Vikram was filling in. There's a catch here. He will definitely have no loyalty towards his master. Therefore it'll be much easier to use him.

And that's where I spot trouble. Let's see. We can't say much till some more time passes by.'

'Suppose something really happens?'

Keshtoda sighed and said, 'I don't know. We need to keep our mouth shut till Jogu is at work. If the stone is stolen, the police will surely come. If the police suspect Jogu Ustad, let them—there's nothing we can do. But if that happens, your film will face huge losses. If need be the police will arrest the culprit, no one can stop that. I'm worried about the film. As far as I know a lot of work involving Jogu Ustad and you remains to be done.'

'Yes, that's true. After I am kidnapped there are three shots with me inside their den. They are torturing me; not feeding me well. I need to survive for days in the same clothes—none of these scenes have been shot.'

'Hmm . . .'

I was touched by Keshtoda's genuine concern for the film.

That one really had reasons to worry became clear on the morning of the eighth day.

We had a schedule in the palace at 9 a.m. It involved a scene between the manager and me. The police had begun their search, while the prince, Amrit, was getting increasingly restless to get the latest news of his new friend. In the absence of any response from the adults, he himself calls up the inspector to ask. Shooting this bit shouldn't take more than an hour or so. The rest of the day's work would be done in the villains' den.

By 7.30 a.m. the bus left along with a few people and the baggage. Bishuda also left with them. The rest would follow by car at 8 a.m. I noticed within twenty minutes that Bishuda returned in an autorickshaw. A major mishap had taken place at the palace. Dacoits had attacked it last night. Striking Mr Lohia on his head and rendering him unconscious, they had taken the key from under his pillow and then the lapis lazuli from the chest. Mr Lohia's wife slept in the next room along with her two grandsons. She had remained unaware of any untoward activity. When Mr Lohia regained his senses, he woke up his wife and explained everything to her.

Bishuda also informed them that one of their retainers, Vikram, could not be found. He had been working as a replacement for the chief bearer, Shatrughan, for a month. The cops had already arrived and had started their investigations. Three days of work were yet to be completed at the palace which would be done at the end of the shooting schedule—after all other work had been done.

In a rush I went down and heard the first-hand account from Bishuda. Keshtoda too was in the room. He glanced once in my direction. I knew that there was nothing we could do now yet we had known about this all along.

Out of the entire team of twenty-five people only Keshtoda and I knew the truth—we knew where and with whom the lapis lazuli was at present.

IX

We completed shooting at the villains' den by 4.30 p.m. On our way back, Bishuda said, 'Come on, Angshu, let us visit Mr Lohia once. We must find out how he is.'

Bishuda, Sushilbabu, Shankar Mallik, Sukantababu and I left for the palace in one car.

There were police inside as well as outside the palace—the palace scenario had changed completely. All the members of the house looked grim. There was stillness in the air, each one talking in whispers—it looked as if the entire house was engulfed in some sorrow. And to top it all the day was cloudy too.

Thank god for small mercies—the injury suffered by Mr Lohia was not very serious. He was sitting in an easy chair on the front verandah, his head bandaged, sipping fruit juice. After requesting us to sit down he ordered a servant to get sherbet for all of us. Sushilbabu said, 'We won't take much of your time. We are here only to inquire about your well-being.'

'I'm much better,' remarked Mr Lohia. 'Life doesn't always run smoothly. It was fated, who could stop it? What I regret is that of the numerous jewels in my collection, the thief took away my favourite gem.'

'Is one of the servants involved?' Sushilbabu asked.

'As he is absconding one has to assume that. I could never have guessed. He had come as a replacement and was doing quite a good job. Suddenly everything has gone topsy-turvy.

'Is the man really on the run?'

'So it seems. He is not likely to stay back in the city after committing such a heinous crime, is he? What I really feel sorry about is that you couldn't do any of your work today. My office-bearers stopped it. Had I known I wouldn't have allowed them to do so. If you want please come tomorrow morning. It won't bother me.

'There's no need for that,' Sushilbabu said. 'You need to get well first. In the interim we will finish our work elsewhere.'

Soon after we finished our sherbet we got up. When we returned to the circuit house it was past 6. Back in my room, as I was thinking of taking a bath, Keshtoda arrived. He looked concerned.

'What's the matter, Keshtoda?'

'Can you tell me how many days of work I'm left with?' Keshtoda asked.

I said, 'Till the 24th. But why?'

'Does Jogu Ustad have work after the 24th?'

'No. His work will be over on 24th morning. He will leave on the evening of the same day.'

'Are you sure?'

'Our schedule is displayed on the drawing-room wall. It will provide you with all the details. But why do you want to know?'

'Because it'll be difficult if I have to leave before his work gets over. I can't open my mouth while he is engaged here.

I need to do whatever I can before he leaves on the 24th. I'll be left with only a few hours. It's going to be very tricky.'

I could jolly well comprehend Keshtoda's worries. In a gesture of regret he shook his head and said, 'Do you know where the trouble lies? There's no guarantee that they'll believe what I've to say.'

I was about to sympathize with Keshtoda but couldn't. Another figure had appeared in the verandah.

Jogu Ustad.

'I see you two are as thick as thieves!' Jogu Ustad said with a crooked smile. 'Dear friend, it's you who'll call for all the clapping in the hall; we deserve nothing but pity. But yes, I have to admit that both of you are delivering first-class performances. Master Angshu is beyond compare and the stuntman is fantastic.'

I said, 'What are you saying, Joguda! Tickets get sold simply thanks to your presence in a film.'

Jogu Ustad suddenly swelled up in arrogance.

'I've been acting as a villain for the last eleven years. One needs real calibre to do that, do you understand, brother Keshto—this is not just tumbling about. Good acting and gymnastics are not the same thing.'

Smiling, Keshtoda spoke in a gentle voice, 'Have I ever denied that, Ustadji? Your name will appear boldly in the title sequence. My name won't be mentioned at all. There's absolutely no difference between my work and that of a labourer.'

Jogu Ustad had not expected Keshtoda to be so self-effacing. Hence, he looked a bit flummoxed. Switching over to a different topic, he said, 'Do you know what I regret, Master Angshu—such a grand stone has gone missing and I couldn't see it even once. I only kept hearing about it from you. Of course one knows who has taken it.'

'What do you mean?' I couldn't help but ask him directly.

'That servant, Vikram, is a scoundrel of the first order.'

'How do you know?' I couldn't follow what Jogu Ustad was leading up to.

'How will I not know?' said Jogu Ustad. 'We end up meeting all sorts of people at the liquor shop. The fellow had come to the shop one day. He tried to involve me. High on the hooch, you know what he told me? "My master owns a valuable gem. If I bring it to you how much will you offer me?" He thought that as I was an actor, I would definitely be a millionaire. I'd just started drinking and so my mind was sharp still. I took him outside the shop, pulled at the amulet tied round his neck, dragged his head near my face and told him, "If I hear you say this one more time, I'll report you straight to the police."'

'You should have done that,' said Keshtoda. 'The scandal could have been avoided.'

'That stone is no longer with him,' said Jogu Ustad. 'He has smuggled it out to somebody for a hefty commission and is now absconding. If the cops have any sense, they should raid all traders who deal in jewels. If these people chance upon a gem like that at such a low rate they'll just lap it up. The stone perhaps costs rupees twenty lakhs. Vikram would give it up if he received only 2000 rupees. How much would a mere servant's demand be?'

After finishing his spiel, he wished us goodnight and left. I looked at Keshtoda in surprise.

'What do you make of this, Keshtoda?'

Keshtoda looked downcast. He looked one way, then the other, and sighed. 'I'm now thoroughly confused. At times I feel as if I'd heard it all wrong. That would have been so much better. If it is proved that Jogu Ustad has taken the stone from Vikram, the reputation of film actors will get tarnished. And that's not nice.'

'No, certainly not.'

X

After this incident I fumbled over my words quite a few times and the shots became 'NG'. NG means no good. Which means the shot needed a retake. If the shot is right it becomes OK. The moment a shot is over, the director tells you if it was OK or NG.

In fact, Sushilbabu once asked me, 'Angshu, are you not feeling well?' Even though he spoke very politely I felt deeply embarrassed. It was really nothing but I couldn't get over the lapis lazuli episode and it affected my concentration. Jogu Ustad's words kept coming back to me. My mind was telling me that Jogu Ustad was innocent. What he was saying was right and what Keshtoda had heard was gibberish.

It took me two days to get over the incident and concentrate on my acting. After this I did not give any NG takes.

Inspector Maheshwari is under pressure regarding the investigation. The servant has obviously left the city but the police force has failed to locate where exactly he has gone into hiding.

On the morning of the 23rd, I had to shoot in 'Mohan's house'. Inspector Suryakant has rescued Mohan from the clutches of the hooligans and has handed over the child to his father. The father takes him in his arms.

Mr Maheshwari had brought along his wife and daughter to watch us shoot. Replying to Bishuda he said that they hadn't caught the thief yet. 'But we have gathered evidence that Vikram is not innocent. On the pretext of going to the market he would go to the liquor shop and consume alcohol. He had visited the shop even on the day the stone was stolen.'

The next day, the 24th, was a crucial one. We would be shooting Keshtoda crossing the canal on his motorbike with me riding pillion. Two extra cameras along with their operators had arrived from Bombay for this. As a room was now vacant in the circuit house they had checked into that. Since it would be risky to shoot the sequence more than once, three cameras have been positioned at different vantage points to capture the scene. The first camera would shoot the bike riding uphill on one side of the canal, the second while it jumps over the canal and the last one will capture the bike landing on the opposite side of the canal.

Prior to this, there were other scenes to be shot in the morning. It required three hooligans and a team of police.

The scene to be shot was that of the police arresting Chhaganlal and party. Inspector Maheshwari had helped us with the local police force that would perform in the scene. Now I'm convinced that Keshtoda had heard wrong. Jogu Ustad was innocent. Vikram had tried to incite him but he didn't fall for it. Thank goodness! It would have been terrible if one had put the blame on Jogu Ustad.

There was one problem: the day was rather cloudy. But a strong breeze ensured that the sun broke through the dark clouds every now and then. We definitely needed the sun in the evening for the scene at the canal as the sun had been visible in the previous shots there.

I had finally got the hang of continuity. If ten shots have been taken against the backdrop of the sun for a scene, and suddenly one shot appears against a cloudy backdrop, it would jar. Therefore since morning I had been praying to God for the clouds to disappear and the sun to come out brightly by evening.

After lunch we set off in one car with Keshtoda, two make-up men and me. The other car carried the two new cameras with the cameramen and an assistant. Others had already left early in the morning to shoot the scene with the criminals. They would reach the canal directly from there.

On our way I spotted Jogu Ustad and some other men returning to the circuit house in car number 3 after completing their shooting. This indicated that Chhaganlal's work was now over.

Like the other day this time too it took us twenty minutes to reach the canal. The motorbike had already arrived atop a bus. Not wasting any time, Keshtoda climbed on to the bike. Those who had come earlier were having puri-sabzi for lunch. Keshtoda said, 'I'll cross over the canal once just to work out my speed.'

I asked, 'Will I be needed?'

Keshtoda shook his head and said, 'You can join me when we take the shot.'

A little further down the path there was a tamarind tree. A group was having lunch under it. Keshtoda shouted to inform everyone that he would rehearse the shot once. Today was his last day at the shoot and he would return to Bombay after this was over. Maybe we'll never meet again. This thought made me deeply unhappy.

Keshtoda had parked the bike alongside the canal a little away from the road.

'Hope there's no one near the canal?' Keshtoda called out loudly.

Bishuda was serving food. He shouted back to say, 'No, everyone's here.'

I ran towards the edge of the canal to watch the rehearsal. Then I said loudly, 'Come over, Keshtoda.'

Once more that ear-splitting sound, that sudden bursting forth from behind the bushes. That breathtaking leap and then—

But what is this? What happened to the bike after it reached the other side? It was lying flat on the ground right near the uphill path. Keshtoda had been flung off the bike and had fallen inside the bush.

'Bishuda!'

Letting out a scream I crossed over the canal with my shoes and socks on and reached the opposite side.

The motorbike was lying tilted on one side, one of its wheels still rotating. Keshtoda got up from the road, wiping off dust from his body.

'I survived because I'm a stuntman, Angshubabu. Someone else . . .'

'Are you hurt?'

My heart was beating.

'The bush saved me. Otherwise, I would have definitely injured my head.'

'But how did—'

'It's nothing much really. Someone had dug up the road to create a hole and then covered it up with loose soil and scattered some pieces of stone over it. I'm sure you have noticed it. Therefore, when the bike started moving it sunk into the soil.'

Bishuda came running along with the others when they heard me shout. Everyone looked shocked.

'But who did this?' Sushilbabu asked. 'Does anyone hold a grudge against you to endanger your life like this?'

Keshtoda had bruised his cheeks and neck. We were carrying a first aid box with us and applied medicine to his injuries.

Sushilbabu once more inquired, 'Do you have any idea who could have done this to you?'

Keshtoda said, 'I have a hunch . . . but then I will need to speak about many things. All I'm trying to say for now is stop the actor you have on your team, by the name of Jogu Ustad, from leaving for Calcutta.'

This upset Bishuda. He said, 'You can't say something like that with no basis. We must know why you want us to do such a thing. Please elaborate. We can't blame anyone without a good reason. Did you have any confrontation with him?'

Left with no choice, Keshtoda had to disclose everything. Now I knew that Keshtoda was right. Bishuda, however, paid no heed to his words.

'Look here, Captain,' said Bishuda, 'that Jogu Ustad drinks every evening is something we're all aware of. But no one has ever accused him of being a thief. He has been in films for long and is very good at it. No one can deny this. Having arrived from Bombay you can't suddenly accuse a Bengali actor of such a serious offence. We will not put up with this. I'm not convinced about what you heard in the wine shop. How do we know that you're not addicted to drinks yourself?'

Keshtoda said, 'I won't deny that I am an occasional drinker. But as I had once fumbled in one of my stunts, I haven't touched alcohol for the last five years. What I heard is absolutely correct—make no mistake. Today's incident is proof of that. Now it's up to you to believe me. I'm absolutely sure that Jogu Ustad has that stone with him and because I'd overheard him, he has organized this ploy to get rid of me.'

Sushilbabu looked very worried. 'Whatever the case, what I want to know is whether we can use the bike on this road again. We have to take this shot. And that too at this very spot as we know there's no other road that can match this location.'

'There'll be some problems shooting here,' said Keshtoda. 'Only after we fill that hole with firm soil and stones can we shoot again. As this was almost hollow the bike went right through it.'

Within half an hour, after much effort, the hole in the road was evened out. It was 2.30 p.m. Could we shoot now? No, the sky was still overcast. It was getting dark. I wouldn't be surprised if it started raining.

I knew that we could not shoot unless the sun came out. When I found Keshtoda sitting all by himself, I whispered to him, 'Jogu Ustad will leave the circuit house by 5.45 p.m. His train is at 6.30 p.m.'

Keshtoda didn't even reply. I placed my hand on his back to sympathize with him. Bishuda had been very unfair in talking to him like that.

Now Keshtoda spoke, his voice heavy and stern.

'Don't tell me anything. I know it's so foolish to try to help people. Had it been Bombay, people would have paid attention to what I said.'

I feared that Keshtoda might refuse to perform the shot in a fit of rage. Hence out of a sense of duty I asked him, 'Keshtoda, will you complete the rest of your work?'

'Let's see.' Keshtoda turned quiet after saying this.

It did not rain but the clouds remained. As the wind had also stopped blowing, the clouds refused to budge. My eyes kept turning towards the sky. Not only me but everyone in the unit was frequently looking up at the sky, waiting for that one shot to take place. One could figure out the position of the sun; in fact every time the cloud thinned, the brightness surrounded you. Yet the sun refused to surface. Cinematographers use a black piece of glass which they tie up with a string and hang round their neck. Dheeresh Bose was looking up at the sky through that glass time and again.

4.30 p.m.

Suddenly I saw Keshtoda picking up the bike with his hands and carrying it across to the other side of the canal, from where the shot would begin. This gave me some hope. It seemed as if Keshtoda's anger had subsided a bit. Surely, he had reason to be angry. Right after the accident I knew that Jogu Ustad was the root cause of the trouble. After stealing the lapis lazuli, Vikram had handed it over to Jogu Ustad, who had realized that Keshtoda had unravelled the mystery. So, yesterday he must have got a few men to dig up the road and cover it with loose soil. Yet Bishuda did not believe Keshtoda. Nobody else did. Did no one trust his words just because he was only a stuntman?

Meanwhile, I'd changed into Amrit's clothes and much to my relief I saw Keshtoda change into the inspector's uniform after affixing the moustache on himself. Soon after Keshtoda got ready, a few from the group chorused, 'The sun's out!'

Looking up at the sky I noticed that the clouds had disappeared and the sun had appeared in the big blue sky. It should remain like this at least for the next five minutes.

'Cameras ready?'

It was Sushil Mitra yelling.

Three cameras had already been placed in three different locations—on two sides of the road and alongside the canal. Now all three cameramen also got ready.

'Come over, Master Angshu!' called Keshtoda in a solemn voice.

Keshtoda and I climbed on to the bike.

'Please shout at us when the camera begins to roll,' Sushilbabu hollered, 'only then will the bike start.'

This time Keshtoda took the bike even further away. He had not ridden the bike from such a distance earlier.

Will the bike arrive at a greater speed this time? I was keen to find out but there was no time for such questions.

'Is everyone ready?' Sushilbabu shouted.

The three cameramen and Keshtoda replied together, 'Ready!'

Riding pillion, I wrapped my arms tightly around Keshtoda's waist.

'Today I'll increase the speed,' Keshtoday muttered under his breath. 'Hang on to me. No need to fear.'

'Start camera!'

Almost in unison all the three cameramen said, 'Running!'

After four to five seconds we could hear the next instruction.

'Start the bike!'

With a roaring noise the bike took off. I had decided not to close my eyes this time. I wanted to watch everything. Going almost one-and-a-half times faster than the last time the bike jumped over the ascending path at breakneck speed.

As if in an instant the present landscape plunged below me.

The bike was now up in the air. I could feel the strong gust of the wind against my face.

After travelling through the air the bike had now begun its descent.

The surroundings once more appeared above me.

Now I understood why Keshtoda had increased the speed. The objective was to avoid the ditch and land on solid ground. Keshtoda didn't want to take any risk with me riding behind him.

With a massive jerk the bike landed on the ground.

I heard from a distance a loud shout: 'OK!'

And soon after, twice more, 'OK.'

Which meant that all three cameras had captured the shot well.

But why wasn't the bike coming to a halt?

Where was Keshtoda heading?

The moment the question came to my head so did the answer.

Whatever Bishuda may have said, Keshtoda was now working on his own.

The canal was 14 kilometres away from the circuit house. The bike reached Ajmer in just ten minutes. Keshtoda stopped the bike next to a traffic signal and asked the man on duty where the nearest police station was.

Once the policeman had given the directions the bike sped off once more. At what speed was the bike running? 80? 90? I had no idea. All I know is that I'd never travelled in any vehicle at such a speed. Due to the sound of the wind I could hear almost nothing else and there were goosebumps on my skin.

Finally we were at the police station.

Within three minutes we met with Inspector Maheshwari. The gentleman recognized me. And he began to laugh when he saw Keshtoda in police uniform.

'What're you looking for?'

'Lohiaji's stone,' said Keshtoda. 'I know where it is. Please follow me in a jeep. If I am wrong, you can put me behind bars.'

Perhaps the conviction in Keshtoda's voice made Mr Maheshwari agree readily.

'All right. I'm coming with you.'

'Please bring along a search warrant.'

'Okay.'

After sitting on the bike I turned over Keshtoda's wrist to look at his watch. Ten minutes to 6. Jogu Ustad must have already set off for the station.

It was dark outside. The city was now lighting up.

Avoiding the traffic on the street, Keshtoda was riding towards the station at lightning speed. A police jeep was behind us, trying to keep up with the bike, frequently blowing its horn to steer the crowd away from the middle of the street.

We arrived at the station in a jiffy. What was the time now? It was not even five minutes since we had left the police station.

Both the bike and the jeep stopped side by side in front of the station.

'There goes Jogu Ustad!' I screamed.

That's true. He too had just arrived at the station. He was placing his luggage over a coolie's head after stepping out of an autorickshaw.

'That is the man!' Keshtoda pointed his finger at Jogu Ustad to draw Maheshwari's attention to him.

Maheshwari proceeded towards Jogu Ustad, carrying a revolver in his hand.

Jagannath Dey aka Jogu Ustad tried to make a dash for it at the last moment but could not. The police surrounded him from all sides. Needless to add, Mr Lohia's lapis lazuli was recovered from him. Mr Lohia was so pleased to get back his priced gem that he decided to offer an amount of Rs 2000 as a token of thanks to Keshtoda. I knew he deserved it. It was true that he was a stuntman but it was also a fact that Keshtoda had never before performed a stunt like retrieving a gem.

If someone was most regretful it was Bishuda. 'I've spoken so harshly to you. It was all a mistake. Hope you'll take no offence.'

'Of course I won't,' said Keshtoda, 'because having worked in this film, in particular with Master Angshuman, I'm really very happy.'

'I want to tell you one thing,' said Bishuda.

'Please do.'

'The names of stuntmen never ever appear in the opening credits. I promise you this time your name will appear in the credits of our film prominently.'

'In that case you will fulfil my long-cherished ambition,' said Keshtoda.

We were at the station. Keshtoda was leaving for Bombay. We had come to bid him goodbye. We would all leave tomorrow evening after finishing a few shots in the morning. Keshtoda turned towards me. He stretched out his right hand, shook hands with me and said, 'I've been working as a stuntman over the past ten years—this is as banal as eating and sleeping. But you are only twelve years old . . . the courage you showed in your first film, this stunt, remains matchless.'

'But when do we meet again, Keshtoda?'

'The day the film releases. I'll buy my own ticket with Mr Lohia's money and come over to Calcutta. Otherwise, it's not possible to watch Bengali films in Bombay.'

The train blew its whistle. In a swift move Keshtoda boarded the coach.

'Goodbye, Master Angshu. Hope you've kept my address?'

'Oh yes.'

'Please write to me.'

The train started moving.

'Of course I'll write to you, Keshtoda. Of course I will.'

Till the train moved out of sight, I could see Keshtoda standing on the step of the coach, holding on to a rod with one hand and with the other waving me goodbye.

10

Rocket[*]

Jayanta Nandy: Editor of a children's magazine, *Rocket*
Tarun Sanyal: Jayanta's friend
Teenkori Dhara: A writer
Raghunath Mutsuddi: An office-bearer at *Rocket* who collects advertisements
Tanmay Sengupta: A writer
Mukul: A worker in the office
Dhananjay/Alam: A peon in the office
Ardhwendu Roy: Father of a subscriber

In Ballygunge. Office of Rocket magazine. A table in the middle of the room. Editor Jayanta Nandy sits in a chair behind the table. He is thirty-five. On the other side of the table are two more chairs. His friend Tarun Sanyal is sitting in one. Alam, the

* First published in *Sandesh*, 1986

PEON, CAN BE SEEN IN ONE CORNER OF THE ROOM, SHOVING THE NEW ISSUE OF ROCKET INSIDE BROWN ENVELOPES. AT THE REAR OF THE STAGE, THERE IS A CLOSED DOOR IN THE MIDDLE. IT'S CLEAR THERE'S ANOTHER ROOM BEHIND IT. NEXT TO THE DOOR IS AN EMPTY CHAIR. THERE IS ONE TEACUP EACH IN FRONT OF JAYANTA AND TARUN.

TARUN: So you're doing pretty well, right?
JAYANTA: Well, we've a subscription of thirteen thousand and the stalls manage to sell another four thousand. How can we say we're badly off? And we cover our costs straight from the advertisements. This month we're carrying four advertisements, out of which two are regular and two occasional. Even our printing is better. The previous press wasn't too good. I changed to a new one last May. See how smart the magazine looks now.

JAYANTA PICKS UP A COPY OF *ROCKET* FROM THE TABLE AND GIVES IT TO TARUN. TARUN LEAFS THROUGH IT.

JAYANTA: You have a flair for writing. Why don't you write for our magazine?
TARUN: Do you pay the writers?
JAYANTA: Yes, indeed. And not a small amount. One hundred rupees for one story, and five hundred if it's a novel. Of course, the rate may vary depending on whether the writer is well known or new.

Tarun: You've chosen such a wonderful name, 'Rocket'. Very attractive.

Jayanta: For the annual issue, I've received a novel by a completely unknown writer called Nabarun Chatterjee. You don't normally get to find such a talented writer. I am in complete awe. But he lives in Bagbajar, otherwise I could have called him over and met him personally.

Tarun: What kind of novel is it?

Jayanta: Adventure. The characters, the atmosphere, the suspense—they're all amazing. It's based in Ladakh. Either this fellow has been there or he's done a lot of homework before writing the novel. I was overwhelmed after reading it.

There is a knock on the office door on the right, which faces the road. A squat, bald-headed, innocent-looking gentleman is standing at the doorway in a rust kurta and short dhoti. His name is Teenkori Dhara.

Teenkori: Is this the *Rocket* office?

Jayanta: Yes, sir. It is.

Teenkori: I've some work with the editor.

Jayanta: I'm the editor. What can I do for you?

Teenkori: I can elaborate on that if I get to sit and talk to you.

Jayanta: Please come inside.

Teenkoribabu walks into the room.

Jayanta: Please wait in that chair. I'm little busy at the moment.

Teenkoribabu sits in a chair positioned a bit far from the table. With one corner of his dhoti, he wipes his sweat. Jayanta turns back towards Tarun.

Jayanta: Ah, well, as I was saying, now the challenge is to find an artist. We must use powerful visuals for this book, otherwise it might not work. You've a fine collection of books. Would you have anything on Ladakh? A photographic book?

Tarun: I might. I'll check.

Jayanta: If you can lend it to me for a week, I'd appreciate it. Nowadays one can't just fabricate stuff in illustrations. One must illustrate using an authentic reference. The fellow Ashish Mitra has good potential as an artist. If I get the book from you, at least I can relax on that front.

Tarun: The way you describe it, I feel like reading this work right away. I must confess even at our age I love reading stuff written for adolescents.

Entry of Raghunath Mutsuddi. He sits in the chair next to Tarun and wipes away his sweat.

Raghunath: A very successful morning. No need to worry about our annual issue. We're getting six colour advertisements, and we've collected twenty-four black-and-whites so far. Bharat Insurance and Poddar Biscuits have also promised theirs, which may work out.

Jayanta: Did anyone complain about our rates?

Raghunath: No. These days all papers quote more or less the same. Our figure is not higher than anyone else's, hence there's no reason for anyone to grouch.

Jayanta: Will they send their matter on time? Last time they sent the ads late despite assurances. As a result, we had to delay production.

Raghunath: I've repeatedly mentioned it to them. Let's see. Dhananjay, are you there?

From the rear room, one can hear the peon Dhananjay's voice.

Dhananjay: Babu?

Raghunath: Please fix me a quick cup of tea.

Raghunath retreats to the back room.

The writer Tanmay Sengupta enters from the door facing the road.

Tanmay: (To Jayanta) Good morning, sir.

Jayanta: Good morning.

Tanmay: I've come to enquire about my manuscript.

Jayanta: Your novel?

Tanmay: Yes.

Jayanta: Haven't you received it yet? We've already sent it back. You had affixed stamps on the envelope.

Tanmay: Does that mean you didn't like it?

Jayanta: No, sir. Very sorry, but it had several flaws. It wasn't convincing enough. Ten- to twelve-year-old boys don't talk like that, nor possess so much courage. I hope you don't mind, but if we had published it, it might have affected your reputation. I'd attached a note with my comments to the manuscript. We have already published two of your stories. Perhaps we should let this one be.

Tanmay: Does this mean you're not publishing any novels this time?

Jayanta: Indeed, we're publishing one. I can guarantee that no annual issue this year will have one like ours.

Tanmay: Is he a well-known writer?

Jayanta: Not at all. I think this is his first work.

Tanmay: What's his name?

Jayanta: Nabarun Chatterjee. Have you heard of him?

Tanmay: No, I haven't.

Jayanta: I too have only heard his name and read this manuscript. Never met him. He lives all the way off in Bagbajar.

Tanmay: Must say, he is very lucky.

JAYANTA: Not everything works on luck, one must have talent too. Of all the writing for adolescents that I've seen in the recent past, there's no doubt that this one's by far the best.

TANMAY: Let me take your leave now.

JAYANTA: Please do. You'll receive your manuscript in a day or two. It's the Calcutta postal service after all. A letter from Ballygunge takes seven days to reach Shyambazar.

TEENKORIBABU CLEARS HIS THROAT FROM HIS CHAIR.

TEENKORI: Well, hello—

JAYANTA: Please wait a bit longer. We will definitely attend to you.

TEENKORI: No, I mean, if I could get some water . . .

JAYANTA: Dhananjay!

DHANANJAY APPEARS.

DHANANJAY: Babu?

JAYANTA: Please bring this gentleman a glass of water.

DHANANJAY BRINGS THE WATER. THE GENTLEMAN GULPS IT DOWN AND ONCE AGAIN WIPES HIS SWEAT WITH HIS DHOTI. THERE'S A FAN ABOVE JAYANTA'S TABLE BUT THE BREEZE DOESN'T REACH TEENKORIBABU. JAYANTA ONCE AGAIN MOVES HIS ATTENTION BACK TO TARUN.

JAYANTA: I was so busy talking about my magazine, I completely forgot to ask about a key thing. Isn't your niece getting married?

Tarun: Yes, next month. You have to come. I'll send you an invitation.

Jayanta: I'd love to come, but I'm not sure if I'll have the time. I'm so overwhelmed trying to bring out this annual issue.

Tarun: I don't want to hear any of this. You can certainly take out a couple of hours off work for one evening.

Jayanta: What are you saying? I couldn't even watch the latest cricket series on television.

Tarun: You didn't even catch the one-day match?

Jayanta: If I were so lucky . . .

Tarun: Oh no! You missed something major. You don't get to see matches like these every day. The suspense of your novel is no match for them.

Tarun stubs his cigarette in the ashtray.

Tarun: Never mind. I won't take up any more of your time.

Jayanta: Hope you won't forget about writing something.

Tarun: I will write, but will expect some payment. Don't use me just because I'm a friend. Bye.

Tarun leaves the office. Jayanta is about to address Teenkoribabu, but another gentleman enters the office. It's Ardhwendu Roy. Jayanta turns his attention towards him instead.

Jayanta: May I help you?

Ardhwendu: I'm here to subscribe to your magazine for my son. This piece of paper has all the particulars. And here's the money.

Ardhwendu takes out the piece of paper and money from his pocket and gives them to Jayanta.

Jayanta: Thanks. Wait, I'll give you a receipt. Mukul!

A young fellow, Mukul, comes out from the room in the back.

Jayanta: Please give him a receipt. One year's subscription. Here are the particulars.

After taking the piece of paper from Jayanta's hand, Mukul gets busy writing the receipt. Jayanta opens the drawer and puts the money in.

Ardhwendu: You need not send me the magazine by post. I'll come personally to collect it from your office as my own office is very close.
Jayanta: Why don't you take a seat?
Ardhwendu: Thanks. My son was after me to get him a subscription.
Jayanta: How old is he?
Ardhwendu: He just turned ten.

Mukul furnishes the receipt. Ardhwendu takes it and leaves the office. After Mukul goes into the back room, Jayanta turns towards Teenkori.

Jayanta: Have you come to contribute an article?
Teenkori: No, sir.
Jayanta: Then?
Teekori: It's already with you.
Jayanta: Has it been approved?
Teenkori: I still haven't received it back. But after listening to you I have a feeling it's been approved.
Jayanta: I don't understand.
Teenkori: My real name is Teenkori Dhara. But my pseudonym is Nabarun Chatterjee.

Jayanta's eyes pop out.

Jayanta: What are you saying?

Teenkori: It's true.

Jayanta: You wrote that Ladakh-based novel?

Teenkori: That's right. It's a result of real hard work. I had to do a lot of groundwork before writing it.

Jayanta: So very strange. But then, instead of introducing yourself as Nabarun Chatterjee why did you say Teenkori Dhara? How will a name like that ever elicit a response!

Teenkori: That's so true. If I'd written under my real name, you might not have read the manuscript at all. But now that you have liked my writing, I'd rather use my real name. Primarily because if one likes the writing, they won't really bother with the name. Also, my father gave me this name, and the surname is part of my lineage. I needed the name Nabarun Chatterjee only to get your attention. Now there's no need any longer.

Jayanta: Look at me! I kept you waiting for so long without realizing it.

Teenkori: So what? Now when you pressure me to hurry up and submit my contribution, I'll keep you waiting. We'll be even.

Both of them burst into a hearty laughter.

Curtain falls.

11

*A Portrait**

Ranjan Purakayastha is a noted painter in Calcutta. Why just Calcutta? His popularity has spread way beyond Bengal, across the whole of India. He has had exhibitions in Bombay, Madras, Delhi, Bangalore and Hyderabad. Ranjanbabu's income, which is quite substantial, comes from selling his paintings. Last month in Bombay, one of his oil paintings was sold for thirty-five thousand rupees.

The painting style Ranjanbabu has adopted is modern. Very little of the real world can be associated with his work. His human figures look like puppets created by some incapable artisan; the trees resemble the twigs of a broomstick; the clouds in the sky look like floating chunks of meat; and his birds and animals have nothing to do with nature or a zoo. But as today's art connoisseurs

---

* First published in *Sandesh*, 1986

appreciate this kind of approach, Ranjanbabu's earnings have not been affected. Yet I must also add, Ranjanbabu remains unrivalled in creating portraitures of people. Here he doesn't adopt his modern style, the pictures look like real people and the likenesses are rather good too. Due to the nature of his work, Ranjanbabu needs to travel often, and that offers him a good income too. For a life-size oil painting, he charges fifteen thousand rupees, which he plans to increase to twenty-five thousand next year. Even in the age of photographs, a few wealthy people still prefer to have their portraits made, and Ranjanbabu gets to prove his expertise again and again.

One Sunday morning, a gentleman arrives at Ranjanbabu's fancily decorated flat on Richi Road. At a glance, one can tell he is wealthy. Tall and hefty, attired in a raw silk suit, and sporting five rings on five fingers. His appearance is marked by a strapping personality. The gentleman says his name is Bilash Mallik, and he is keen to have his portrait done. When Ranjanbabu hears his name, he knows the gentleman is one of Calcutta's most affluent businessmen. His will be a life-size portrait, and he is ready to pay any amount stipulated.

'How much will you charge?' Mr Mallik asks.

With a straight face, Ranjanbabu says, 'Fifty thousand rupees.'

The client promptly agrees.

Ranjanbabu already has an incomplete work at hand, a large painting. He needs at least seven days to finish it. Accordingly, he calculates his timeframe and offers Mr Mallik a date. He will have to do a one-hour sitting every day at 9 a.m.

'How many days will you take to finish it?' Mr Mallik queries.

'About a fortnight.'

'Very well,' says Mr Mallik. 'It's settled. Hmm . . . do you require an advance?'

'No, sir.'

Before embarking on any major project, Ranjanbabu always seeks his guru's blessings. He became Saralananda Swami's—also known as Babaji or Swamiji—disciple ten years ago. On many occasions he takes Babaji's advice, and the latter too is very fond of this disciple. Babaji has been bestowed with many powers, and fortune-telling is one of them.

After listening to everything his disciple tells him, Babaji meditates for three minutes and then says, 'There is danger.'

'What danger, Swamiji?'

'A lot of mishaps. You didn't do the right thing by taking up this task.'

'Then should I refuse the gentleman?'

'Wait.'

Babaji closes his eyes once again and begins to sway. This continues for another five minutes, after which Babaji finally opens his eyes. Ranjanbabu is looking at his guru reverentially.

'I can foresee you ultimately crossing all the hurdles and finding success. Don't worry; get on with your work,' Babaji says.

Greatly relieved, Ranjan Purakayastha touches Babaji's feet and takes his leave.

The work on Bilash Mallik's portrait commences on Saturday, 21 January. Mr Mallik is a jovial fellow. Right at the outset he checks if he can talk during sittings. Usually Ranjanbabu doesn't permit this, but since this is an exceptional client, he has to say yes.

'But you shouldn't move your neck. If you speak, speak in one direction, that is, look at my right shoulder and then speak.'

When the first stroke of charcoal appears on the canvas, the time is 9.15 a.m.

Day by day, Mr Mallik's face begins to emerge. There's no doubt that Ranjanbabu is a very skilful artist, but at this juncture the only person who can see his work is the artist himself. The person whose portrait is being created will get to see it only after it's completed. Even though this condition wasn't discussed beforehand, Mr Mallik doesn't have any objections.

It's the twelfth day, and the portrait is nearing completion. After half an hour of sitting, Mr Mallik says he's feeling dizzy.

Ranjanbabu stops and says, 'Please go home. In any case, the portrait is almost complete. If you feel better, please come back tomorrow morning.'

But Mr Mallik doesn't feel any better the next day. In fact, his fever goes up to 103 degrees. On the third day, things turn even more serious and he is shifted to a hospital.

Ranjan Purakayastha removes the portrait from the easel, puts it aside and fixes a brand-new canvas on it. Then he starts to work on a landscape with a modern touch.

After spending one-and-a half months in hospital, when Mr Bilash Mallik finally returns home, he no longer carries any resemblance to his former self. He has lost weight—down to seventy-two kilos from ninety. His cheeks are now hollow and his eyes sunken. He sends word to Ranjan Purakayastha that the portrait can wait. When his appearance becomes a little better, he can once again come for a sitting.

A month later, Mr Bilash Mallik begins to look better. Yet there's no resemblance between his former and present selves. Doctors have advised him to control his diet. With the result, his weight can never go beyond eighty kilos.

Mallik says, 'Let's do a new portrait in my present state.'

Ranjan Purakayastha places a fresh canvas on his easel. Mr Mallik has altered his clothes to fit his reduced frame. But it's a fact that he no longer looks unwell.

After four days of sketching, Ranjanbabu goes shopping to New Market in his Fiat one evening. On the way back, as soon as he crosses the turn at Park Street, a mini bus coming at high speed rams into the car from the right.

Of course, the Fiat is damaged, but along with it, Ranjanbabu's right hand is severely battered. In the hospital, the X-ray reveals multiple fractures on his elbow, wrist and the right thumb.

Once the cast on his hand is taken off after two months, Ranjanbabu discovers that he will never regain the same level of artistic expertise as he had before the accident. The most critical issue is his thumb. One can create modern art by holding a brush between the index and middle fingers, but not a natural portrait.

This causes a huge trauma in Ranjanbabu's life. He stops all work and goes on a pilgrimage. After spending three months travelling in Kashi, Haridwar, Rishikesh and Lakshman Jhula, he returns home and starts painting again using two fingers. The work produced looks slack and the appearance of his work completely changes. Ranjanbabu can now no longer demand thirty to forty thousand rupees for a painting. He needs to re-establish his market. Meanwhile, Mr Bilash Mallik enquires about him, extends his sympathies and deeply regrets that he can now no longer have a Ranjan Purakayastha portrait in his house.

After trying for three months, using the paintbrush with only two fingers, Ranjanbabu manages to evolve a style that eventually earns him an endorsement in the art market. One Sunday morning, the retainer comes to his studio to announce the arrival of a gentleman.

'You know him,' the retainer remarks.

Ranjanbabu goes downstairs. His eyes pop out when he enters the drawing room. Is he dreaming? Right in front of him is Mr Mallik looking exactly like his former bulky self.

'What brings you here?' Ranjanbabu asks.

'Nothing really,' Mr Mallik replies. 'I'm a great lover of good food. Couldn't obey the doctor's orders and was unable to control my diet. Therefore, in no time I've turned back into my older version. Hope you haven't destroyed my portrait.'

'No, not at all. But I do need to add a few more strokes, which I should be able to do with my two fingers. Could you come tomorrow for a couple of hours?'

'Certainly, certainly. Well, in the meantime your rate must have gone up, too. I'm willing to pay you more than the amount we had initially discussed for the portrait. I hope you don't mind.'

12

Telephone[*]

Ring, ring, ring, ring!

Bireshbabu glared at the telephone on the table next to his bed. The clock beside the phone showed twelve. It being midnight, Bireshbabu was about to shut the book he was reading and switch off the light.

The telephone continued to ring. Finally, Bireshbabu picked up the receiver.

'Hello?'

'465176?'

'Yes?'

'Is Bireshbabu there? Biresh Chandra Niyogi?'

'Speaking.'

'Oh, ok. Namaskar.'

'Namaskar.'

'Sorry for calling you this late.'

---

[*] First published in the annual issue of *Ananda*, 1987

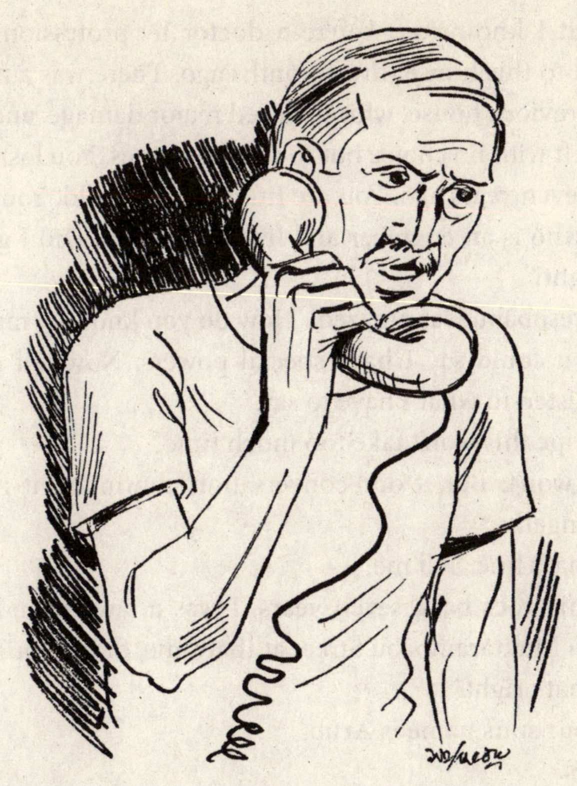

'That's fine. What is it?'

'I'd like to say something to you.'

'May I know who I am speaking with?'

'My name is Ganapati Som.'

Bireshbabu's annoyance doubled. 'I don't have the time to speak with you. I was about to go to sleep. And besides, I don't even know you.'

'But I know you. You're a doctor by profession. You shifted to this house three months ago. There was a fire in your previous house, which caused major damage, and you were left with no choice but to change homes. You lost your wife eleven years ago. You are fifty-five years old. You have a son who is an engineer and lives in Bhopal. Did I get all that right?'

Bireshbabu was amazed. 'How do you know so much?'

'You could say I have special powers. Now tell me if you'll listen to what I have to say.'

'Hope this won't take too much time.'

'It won't. But if our conversation continues, it might take longer.'

'That's fine. Tell me.'

'This goes back seven years. I was a lawyer, and you lived in Muktarambabu Street at that time, didn't you?'

'That's right.'

'Your son's name is Arup.'

'Yes.'

'Was he studying in City College at the time?'

'Yes.'

'Let me see if you know this too. Your son had a friend called Sreepati.'

'It's possible. I wasn't too familiar with my son's friends.'

'Sreepati was my second son. He was such a fine boy. Good in studies too. Your son Arup was the closest among all his friends. Unfortunately, my son fell into bad company.

As a result, he developed a lot of bad habits. Arup tried very hard to dissuade him from associating with those people, but to no avail. Yet Arup's fondness for Sreepati didn't wane. Arup was hell-bent on bringing Sreepati back on the right track, but his efforts didn't bear any fruit. Did you know any of this?'

'I've seen this friend of Arup's, but had no idea about him keeping bad company.'

'Now let me tell you about an unfortunate incident. My son got addicted to gambling. He suffered huge losses and accumulated an enormous debt. He turned to Arup for help. He told Arup that if Arup didn't help him, he would have no choice but to kill himself. Do you know how Arup helped him?'

'Now I understand.'

'What do you understand?'

'There's a chest in my house that belonged to my grandfather. It contained a diamond ring.'

'Yes. Your grandfather was the family physician for the king of Chandipur state. He had saved the raja from an incurable illness, and the raja had gifted him this ring in gratitude. Am I right?'

'Yes.'

'Your son took the ring from the chest and gave it to my son.'

'How strange! None of us could solve the mystery of the missing ring. Not even the police.'

'How could they? You son is so sensible and solemn, how could anyone have suspected him?'

'Yes, of course.'

'My son took such a liking to the ring that he decided to keep it. He didn't want to part with it. When I came to know about my son's money troubles, I turned to a moneylender and helped him clear his debts.'

'Is the ring still with your son?'

'Yes, but now he wants to give it back to you. He has finally got over his attachment. By returning it to you, he wants to redeem his sins.'

'Is your son in a hurry to meet me?'

'Yes—and right away. He has already left for your house. He may have even reached.'

'What did you say his name is?'

'Sreepati.'

'And your name is Ganapati?'

'Yes.'

'Haven't your names appeared in the newspaper recently?'

'Yes, indeed.'

'Wait a minute. Let me remember.'

'Please take your time.'

After giving it a little thought, it hit Bireshbabu. 'I remember now. Your names had appeared in yesterday's paper.'

A driver and two passengers in a car were killed when the car collided with a truck on Barrackpore Trunk Road. The two passengers were a father, Ganapati Som, and his son, Sreepati Som.

'You're absolutely right. I'm the same Ganapati Som.'

'Y-y-you . . . which means . . .'

'Which means what you're thinking is right.'

'But this is impossible!'

'Why should it be impossible? Please listen carefully, can you hear any sound?'

'Yes, I can.'

'What is it?'

'Someone is knocking on my main door downstairs.'

In the quiet of the night, it was the only thing Bireshbabu could hear. Knock. Knock. Knock.

And then, on the telephone, the voice said, 'Open the door. My son is waiting.'

'No. No, I won't open the door.'

Bireshbabu's throat was parched. His hand holding the receiver trembled.

The voice on the telephone said, 'Even if you don't open the door, he can still come inside. He has that power. Listen again.'

Bireshbabu heard footsteps approaching the staircase.

'Please put your worries to rest, Bireshbabu. He won't disturb you. He will simply go to the next room and place the ring on the table.'

In sheer terror, Bireshbabu called out, 'No, no! Please call your son back! Call your son back!'

'There's no such option, Bireshbabu. He has reached the second floor.'

Bireshbabu could clearly hear footsteps in the next room. They paused for a moment, then started again. Then they could be heard going down the stairs.

The voice on the telephone said, 'You can relax now. Put down the telephone and check the next room. I bid you adieu. It was nice talking to you. Goodnight.'

Bireshbabu put the receiver down. Even in the month of January, sweat beaded his face. He sat on his bed for a while and then got up. With great trepidation, he walked towards the next room, opened the door and switched on the light.

It was indeed lying on the table. Even in the dim light, it sparkled. His grandfather's diamond ring, back where it belonged, after seven years.

Translator's Note

One of the fondest memories of my childhood is staring in awe at the top shelf of our bookcase teeming with bound volumes of Sandesh. It had been de rigueur to read Sandesh after finishing the mandatory homework. I'd drag a stool to stand on in my bid to reach for any volume of the magazine. It hadn't just been the lure of a Shonku exploit or a Feluda adventure, but ultimately it had also been the desire to discover the writer's enormous range of short stories, each one completely different from the next, which would always leave me longing for more. What had turned his short stories into a diehard addiction for me? The unique amalgamation of the twisted plot, atypical characters, the language brimming with gentle humour, and the mind-blowing black-and-white illustrations—all of these elements had left me spellbound every time. That had been my first introduction to Satyajit Ray. Much later I was to discover him as a filmmaker.

I imagine this man sitting upright in a chair, feet propped up on the table a writing pad on his knees, creating characters and telling stories, the likes of which readers of Bengali had never known before. The strangest thing is that Ray didn't start writing fiction until he was forty. It was only after he revived Sandesh that his first writings were published. The magazine was founded by his grandfather Upendrakishore Ray Chowdhury in 1913, who left this legacy to his son Sukumar who nurtured it until his untimely death in 1923 at the age of thirty-six. After a few years, the publication of Sandesh ceased.

The magazine's revival in 1961 was nothing short of revolution. No one knew then that by doing so, Ray had set a new milestone not only in his own life but also in the literature of Bengal.

Ray knew he was writing for young readers, but there was never an attempt to oversimplify or talk down to them. He spoke elegantly, yet simply. Never as a young reader did I have to consult a dictionary. Difficult words, facts and concepts that a reader might not be familiar with were explained with great clarity. In fact, what he wrote was undeniably devoured by young and old alike.

There are dozens of stories with the recurring motif of a bachelor living with just a servant for company. Some of these have a hint of the supernatural. Others deal with human relations and frailties. Each is a new and enthralling experience.

In an interview with Aparna Sen, Ray says, 'I think I've written enough on films and on other topics. Right now I only want to concentrate on writing short stories. I find this most satisfying. It offers me the most interesting process. Plotting, structuring, stimulating characters, particularly those who are loners. Living alone—often with certain preoccupations. I find this most engaging. I'm obsessed with loners.'

Another obsession one notices in his writings is the development of characters who mostly appear from the 'lower rungs of society'. Elaborating on this, Ray says, 'In general, those who are well educated, a bit upper caste, their activities and problems don't appeal to me at all. What joy it gives me to write about these simplistic, down to earth individuals.'

Each of these above-mentioned traits can be found in this present collection. Yet, this is a collection with a difference. It opens with a story about which Ray categorically remarks in an interview with Dhritiman Chaterji, 'My only story written strictly for the adults.' He then carries on to explain with great eloquence the essence of this loaded story titled 'The Life and Death of Aryasekhar'. Ray's cardiologist Dr Bakshi had once professed that there's a definite design, a superior force that works in the functioning of the entire human body. Ray had begged to differ as he had a different theory on the matter. For him this story is possibly a way to refute Dr Bakshi's theory. Written in 1964, in immaculate classic Bengali, it's a complete departure from his usual repertoire. A story like this needs to be read many times to fully comprehend its multiple layers. It's a rare treat for curious souls.

In complete contrast follows a story so coated in whimsy that the plot leaves one completely baffled. Laced with humour that needs to be decoded in every line, it revolves around the quirky Professor Hijibijbij whose monologues and activities have one either in splits or extremely worried. The story serves as a wonderful ploy by Ray to pay homage to his father. It's peppered with references to Sukumar's writings, and unless one is familiar with the latter's works like Abol Tabol and Ha-ja-ba-ra-la, a reader can never fully indulge in these allusions. As an aid to those who are uninitiated in the works of Sukumar Ray, I've provided a list of annotations at the end of the story. Translating this was indeed a hugely challenging task.

Another highlight of this collection is a long short story that will hold every reader's attention till the last page. It narrates a nail-biting adventure an adolescent boy finds himself in after arriving at a film shoot where he plays the double role of a rich boy and a poor boy. Responding to the demands of the plot, Ray builds in all the nuances and logistics that go into shooting a film. A young reader will definitely view films with a new enjoyment and understanding after reading this story. As icing on the cake, this adventure is now being made into a feature film.

Elements of the macabre, supernatural, eerie, open-ended conclusions as well as human oddities have always made an inroad into Ray's plots. And this collection offers you all of that and more. For some of Ray's stories, defining the real target reader is extremely difficult. A case in point being 'Worthless', a pithy and extremely moving story about a hapless character who overtly appears to be worthless, but by the end of the story, one can't help but wonder if he isn't a bit like you and me. A story certainly aimed more at adults yet so different in mood from the opening story.

'The McKenzie Fruit' is another moving narration that talks of human failings. The protagonist of the story, the self-effacing Nishikantababu, discovers a mysterious fruit in a garden. But his humble approach to disseminate the news about this discovery goes awry when his astute and greedy 'friends' instantly sideline him. But Nishikantababu's own reaction isn't of resentment or anger but of letting go. This, I strongly believe, was Ray's own outlook on life.

One story reiterates Ray's strongly held anti-colonial viewpoint and revolves around a fervent Anglophile. A treat to read, 'The First-Class Compartment' is perhaps the outcome of the nationalistic milieu in which Ray grew up. The eerie connection between different periods, trains and a ghost could not have been narrated more evocatively.

There are four short stories in the collection that are indeed very short but offer a solid punch in the end. Interestingly, one of these is written in the form of a play.

In the original Bengali, Ray compiled his short stories into seven volumes, the names of which are a play on the words 'twelve' or 'a dozen'. Each jacket makes use of elegant typographical art to showcase the titles. Alas, there can never be an English equivalent of this.

As always, I must not forget to thank Sohini Mitra of Puffin Books along with her competent team for producing this volume. Thanks also to Sandip Ray for providing us with the original illustrations of each story by Satyajit Ray. Finally, I thank my brother Jyotirmoy Majumdar, who introduced me to Sandesh and Satyajit Ray.

With this volume, I pay homage to Satyajit Ray, the writer, on his centenary year. If it manages to give its readers the same joy that I had felt when reading the stories in the original, the credit should go entirely to the author.

I dedicate this book to the memory of my sister, Gopa Majumdar, whose translations will always remain a hard act to follow.

Indrani Majumdar
March 2021

***Indrani Majumdar** is a researcher firmly rooted in the Bengali culture. Her explorations have included studying the various facets of Satyajit Ray's work, as well as translating several texts from Bengali into English and vice versa. She lives and works in Delhi.*

PUFFIN CLASSICS

Another Dozen Stories

With Puffin Classics, the story isn't over
when you reach the final page.
Want to discover more about
the author and his world?
Read on . . .

CONTENTS

AUTHOR FILE

NAME: Satyajit Ray

BORN: 2 May 1921, in a progressive Brahmo family of Kolkata

FATHER: Sukumar Ray, famous writer, poet and printing technologist

MOTHER: Suprabha Ray

QUALIFICATIONS: BA in Economics (Hons) from Presidency College, Kolkata. Trained in Oriental Arts for three years at Visva-Bharati University

PROFESSIONAL LIFE: Worked in the advertising agency DJ Keymer for almost twelve years. Started as a junior visualizer and went on to become the art director

MARRIED TO: Bijoya Ray

CHILDREN: One son, Sandip Ray, also a film-maker

FAMOUS FOR: Internationally acclaimed films. One of the earliest Indian directors to have won prizes at major film festivals around the world like Cannes, Venice, Berlin, London and San Francisco. An extremely versatile person, he wrote the script, composed the music, designed the sets and costumes, prepared posters in addition to directing the films. Ray was also a writer of repute, and his short stories, novellas, poems and articles, written in Bengali, are still immensely popular. Many of his books became bestsellers. He also illustrated them.

MAJOR AWARDS: Bharat Ratna, highest civilian award of India; Legion D'Honneur, highest civilian award of France; and the Oscar for Lifetime Achievement

THE TWELVE STORIES SERIES

Apart from the stories about detective Feluda and Professor Shonku the scientist, Satyajit Ray wrote 91 short stories. This includes his first 2 stories, written in his early twenties originally in English, 4 fairy tales and 13 stories featuring the storyteller, Tarini uncle. Most of his stories were for children and were first published in children's magazines like *Sandesh* and *Anandamela*. Subsequently, they were printed as collections of twelve stories. This book is a translation of the second collection *Aro Ek Dojon* (Another Dozen), which is a follow up book to *Ek Dojon Goppo* (One Dozen Stories) also published by Puffin Books.

After this, the titles of the collections were interesting wordplays on the Bengali word for twelve (*baro*): *Aro Baro* (Twelve More), *Ebaro Baro* (Twelve Again), *Bah! Baro* (Wow! Twelve) and *Jobor Baro* (Solid Twelve) were names of subsequent collections.

Another book in the series was *Eker Pithey Dui* (Two On One). This title was taken from a poem by Ray's father Sukumar Ray. (A translation of the full poem is available in the book *Wordygurdyboom! The Nonsense World of Sukumar Ray*, also published by Puffin India in the Puffin Classics series.)

Were these stories ever made into films?

Ray himself adapted and expanded two of his stories for his films. One took place in the form of a screenplay which got foiled and never took off. The story was 'Bonkubabu's Friend' and the screenplay was titled, *The Alien*. The other story 'The Stranger' turned out to be the film that was his swansong, *Agantuk* (The Stranger).

Each of Ray's short stories have a tight plot and end with a nice twist in the tale. When his son Sandip Ray made the television serial *Satyajit Ray Presents* he took most of the stories from his father's works. The serial was made in two parts. In the first part, there were thirteen short stories—one per episode—and was televised in 1985. A second part had two long stories and a Feluda novella, all based on Ray's writings.

Satyajit Ray Presents was similar in nature and style to the famous American series of the 1950s and 1960s, *Alfred Hitchcock Presents*. These were half-hour episodes of mystery, suspense, crime and drama which were typical of the Hitchcock style of storytelling. The show was voted by *Time* magazine as one of 'The 100 Best TV Shows of All Time'. Alfred Hitchcock—maker of suspense masterpieces like *Psycho* and *Rebecca*—also did not direct the series and only introduced it in a humorous style. He once said, 'The television is bringing back murder to its rightful setting—the living room.'

Indian cities and towns in Satyajit Ray's works

A hallmark of Ray's stories and novels is the accuracy in the description of the settings. Interestingly, almost all the settings were places where he had shot his films. Since shooting a film required extensive knowledge of the terrain, he used these details when he created the backdrop for his stories.

He shot in rural West Bengal for several of his films like *Pather Panchali* (1955), *Abhijan* (1962) and *Goopy Gyne Bagha Byne* (1968). Of course, the city of Calcutta, where he lived and worked, featured prominently in his works.

Locales in Ray's stories have always played a crucial role. Ray, through his characters and plots, has always discreetly imparted layers of information about the city the story is based on. In this present collection, other than his beloved city Calcutta, the other cities used as backdrops are Gopalpur in Orissa; *Daltonganj in Jharkhand, Karimganj in Assam; Raipura in Madhya Pradesh; Rourkela in Odisha; and Ajmer, Pushkar and Doural in Rajasthan.*

THINGS TO THINK ABOUT

Satyajit Ray's stories cut across several genres and cover a wide variety of topics. The twelve stories in this collection are about very different things. Here is a list of the topics, a piece of trivia and something to think about each.

1. In the story 'The Life and Death of Aryasekhar', Aryasekhar frets about who his ancestors were and he realizes that the creation of a family tree would answer his questions. The idea of studying genealogy and documenting it is very interesting as well as important. Why don't you start working on a family tree starting with your own family?
2. Having read the bizarre story of a strange man with pointy ears, would you assist Professor Hijibijbij in his practice of plastic surgery?
   Just as the story mentions storcoise (stork + tortoise), porcochard (pochard + porcupine) or gizzard (parakeet + lizard), you could also mix up some other animals and birds and pair them in these peculiar combinations, name them and, as a further step, make sketches of them.
3. Wherever you travel always look out for landscapes and the greenery around you and observe individual trees, bushes, fruits, flowers and try to find out their local as well as Latin names. And when travelling quietly, notice people and their activities. It can be a wonderful exercise to sharpen your sense of observation. Besides, such knowledge of the world around you could help you escape a fate such as that of Jaganmaybabu in the story 'The Poisonous Flowers' or even discover a new species like the McKenzie fruit!
4. Railways can be a fascinating subject to study. Starting from steam engines of the 17th century to bullet trains you can find

out the intricacies and logistics of running a train, which could even turn out to be a lifetime passion. What kind of train was it that Rajanbabu was so fond of in the story 'The First Class Compartment'?

5. Samaresh Brohmo in 'A Hoax' is passionate about his books, so much so that he has his very own library, complete with a lending system! Wouldn't it be fun to create a library of your own in your house? To start with, learn to catalogue books. You can start arranging your collection of books according to subject, author or title. Another exciting activity for you to pursue is to try your hand at tricks and magic. You can start with playing cards.
6. In the story, Ramdhan mentions that his flute had gotten better with age and produced better music. I wonder if we can change this to an exercise where readers can find out whether wooden flutes (and perhaps other music instruments too – I've heard this about violins too) truly sound better with age, and why.
7. Who isn't fond of watching films? But have you ever thought of all the planning, procedures and paraphernalia that go into making a film? The story 'Master Angshuman' in this book gives you an idea of the many people and processes involved. If you were to make your own film, how would you plan it? You could first make a list of cast and unit members, the equipment and costumes you might need, prepare a shooting schedule, etc.
8. Now that you have your lists and plan in place, how about writing a one-act play and put on a production with your friends? You can refer to the story 'Rocket' for ideas on how to write a play and set the stage for it.

   Another creative challenge can be to make your own handwritten magazine. You can be the editor and request

your friends or cousins to form a group and contribute in such a journal.

9. Have you ever tried sketching or painting faces or portraits? Your model could be your family members, your friends, your pets or even yourself—make a self-portrait.
10. Think of a plot and try your hand at writing a story strictly on the basis of a dialogue between two individuals—like it appears in the story 'Telephone'. Bank on your imagination and go for it!